Redenbaugh

Copyright © 2015 by Sean Redenbaugh

All rights reserved. No part of this publication may be reproduced, distributed, or transmitted in any form or by any means, including photocopying, recording, or other electronic or mechanical methods, without the prior written permission of the publisher and author, except in the case of brief quotations embodied in critical reviews and certain other noncommercial uses permitted by copyright law. For permission requests, write to the publisher, addressed "Attention: Permissions Coordinator," at the address below.

Printed by Ingram Spark / Lightning Source
Printed in the United States of America
2015 Second Edition

First Printing, 2015
ISBN 978-0-692-37764-2

ACKNOWLEDGEMENTS

I would like to express my gratitude to the many people who have helped me; to those who have provided support and inspiration; and to those who have proofread, bounced around ideas, or simply encouraged me along the way.

First and foremost, I thank my Loving parents, for their words of wisdom, their belief in me in anything I chose to do, their joy at my tiniest accomplishment, their Love and guidance, and of course for my very existence. I thank the rest of my family for most of those very same things.

To Amanda, my friend since 2010 and wife since 2014, I Love you, and this book would not exist in its current form without your endless encouragement and enthusiastic support of all my projects and ideas. You have been a blessing in my life.

To all of my friends, who have endured my eclectic and eccentric ways, I thank you for your friendship, your support, and all the good times that make this fleeting life worth living.

To my editor, Cara Lockwood, I thank you for your keen eye, guidance, and encouraging words in this difficult to navigate, frustrating, yet endlessly fulfilling endeavor of writing.

And lastly I would like to thank those who have given me the most inspiration of all, by penning my favorite books of all time and sparking my Love of reading and writing: Aldous Huxley (Brave New World), J.R.R. Tolkein (Lord of the Rings), Yann Martel (Life of Pi), H.G. Wells (The Time Machine), F. Scott Fitzgerald (The Great Gatsby), Victor Hugo (Les Miserables), Daniel Quinn (Ishmael), Dan Brown (The DaVinci Code), George Orwell (1984), Dan Millman (The Way of the Peaceful Warrior), Paulo Coelho (The Alchemist), William Golding (Lord of the Flies), George Orwell, Harper Lee, Michael Blake, Charles Dickens, etc…

SUNLIGHT PARTED

CHAPTER ONE

AWAKENING

Seth awoke. It was slow and gradual, like the changing of the tides, or the breaking of day. His mind gently released its grip on the dreams that were born in him during the night, and bounced through the most vivid images of his latest adventure. He wasn't sure whether he was actually awake yet or still dreaming, and for a second or two he was lost in confusion with no idea where he was. Usually this feeling faded away quite quickly as reality began to set in, but for Seth, on this particular morning, it lingered much longer.

As the images bounced through his head, his mind began to send the message of waking to the individual parts of the body, and his physical senses came to him one by one. With his eyes still closed, having yet to rid themselves of the night, touch was the first sense he noticed. His fingers began to feel blindly beneath him to gather a sense of place and reality. He expected to touch soft cotton sheets, but instead, felt something course, dry, and grainy, and it depressed slightly when his fingers pushed into it. He scooped up a small amount into the palm of his hand and rolled it in his fingers, letting it fall loosely between them. This was no bed sheet or blanket. This was sand. And it was all around him.

Hardly believing it, he called upon his eyes to make sense of the matter, and with a total lack of deliberation, he began to open them. His lids were heavy, and the muscles strained to lift them. It was as if he were doing so for the first time, like a newborn child. *Must have been one hell of a night,* he thought as his eyelids opened.

Still lying on his back, and staring straight above him, Seth saw only darkness. He blinked a few times before convincing himself that his eyes were indeed actually open. He tried again, but above him darkness still prevailed. Then out of the corner of his eye he caught a glimpse of something very bright hovering above him. He turned his head slightly to examine it. There above him, clearly and distinctly, was the moon, floating in the night sky. *I'm outside?*

It took a few seconds for this information to sink in, but when it did, his body stirred. Although slow to wake at first, alertness now suddenly rushed in on him like a wave. All of his senses immediately came to him, and his mind shook off the fog of sleep, ready to uncover the mystery of these new surroundings. *What the hell am I doing outside?*

Seth pulled hard and sat up. The amount of effort it took was much more than he expected. His whole body felt heavy and cumbersome. *How long have I been out? I must have been asleep for a long time.*

As soon as his eyes took in the scenery before him, the strangeness of his situation hit him with a thud. At first, he stared blankly in front of him for several seconds with no expression. He was sitting on a beach.

The sand in front of him swept away for about twenty yards and then disappeared beneath the surface of the water before him. It was a beach he had never seen before, or at least not one that he could remember, and an odd one at that. Everything around him seemed coated in darkness. It was the kind of dark that made the sky feel as if it were a blanket hovering only thirty or forty feet in the air. It was a dark that seemed suffocating and controlling, shutting out all light. The darkness had a presence, almost personified in Seth's mind. The only light he could see was the glow of the full moon above, barely lighting the tips on the water before him, a calm, nearly glassy surface, that seemed to move subtly, if at all. There was no tide, nor any waves, yet he was certain that this was unmistakably the ocean. The smell of salt hung stagnant in the air and seemed to cling to his skin. The water was motionless and dark, and thicker than any water he had ever seen. To Seth, it almost appeared to be oil.

Where am I?

He looked left and right and in every direction, but saw only more darkness. The entire landscape seemed to be like a muted shadow. He saw no houses, no rocks, and no palm trees. Only blank sand as far as he could see. The darkness in this place had certain heaviness to it, and it planted seeds of fear in Seth with every glimpse. A layer of fog and mist hung motionless in the air in every direction. For reasons he could not grasp this morning, his world had shrunk to a few hundred square yards of darkness in every direction.

How did I get here?

He looked up and stared at the familiar moon, the only discernible object he could see. Strangely though, as dark as the sky was, not a single star shared the sky with the moon. It hung alone, reluctantly giving away what little light was borrowed from some unseen force, giving the beach a cold, ominous, and somewhat guilty feeling. The air was cold and heavy here. Every breath seemed to require an effort he wasn't used to, and when the air hit his lungs the cold bit into him from the inside. A shiver went up his spine, perhaps from the cold, and perhaps from the scenery his eyes saw before him. Even the sand underneath him was cold and dry. It fell through his fingers and refused to stick to his skin at all. Each tiny grain simply fell softly and silently back to the earth beneath him, and for all he could tell, back to the exact same spot where it lay before he took it.

As Seth watched the sand fall to the ground, he looked down and for the first time realized he was naked.

What the...?

His skin seemed pale under the light of this strange moon, as did everything before him. In fact, if there were any colors at all, he was unable to see them. He rubbed his eyes in an attempt to clear his view, but everything seemed to be its own unique shade of gray.

What happened last night?

He sat there in the sand facing the water for several minutes trying to come up with an answer, but failed to remember anything of value. He couldn't recall what he did the day before, or what events may have led to the beach. He had no idea what day it was, or month, or year. For some reason he couldn't grasp anything. No facts, no memories, only feelings and emotions swelled within him. He was getting scared and frustrated.

Think! It's what you do best.

Yet his thoughts seemed to be confined to this place and this place alone, leaving him with only confusion and a muddled mind.

Maybe I've been left out here as a joke... but who would do it, and why would they take my clothes?

Maybe I was on a boat that went down, and I washed up on the beach like this...

Maybe I hit my head, which would explain why I can't remember anything.

He instinctively put his hands on his head and felt for wounds or an injury of some kind. He found nothing.

Perhaps I am dreaming all of this...

"I am awake." He said the words aloud, hoping that hearing the sound of his own voice might somehow confirm his statement. Piercing through the extreme silence of this place, his voice sounded deep and powerful, and echoed in his head. He was definitely awake, yet the more he tried to remember, the more he felt as if he were trying to grasp smoke.

It was only after Seth stood up and turned to look around that he saw what was behind him. About fifty yards farther up the beach from where he now stood was a small beach house, nestled in the darkness, and lit only on the facade by the light of the moon. It was no beach house that he could remember, giving him no clue as to where he might be. And this particular beach house was one that he didn't care to know. It had a very strange and surreal feeling about it, and appeared to have been abandoned or forsaken decades ago. The windows, broken and dark, gaped at him like blank eyes. Whatever glass remained in the frames hung like jagged teeth, protecting the dark abyss behind them.

Splintered and peeling strips of dry wood, cracked and broken, covered the house's exterior, like the dried out and shriveled up skin of a long-dead corpse. The door facing Seth hung by a single rusted hinge, crooked and revealing only slivers of the darkness behind it. Leading down to the sand from the door was a small wooden porch and three steps, which had seen better days. The battered railing lay alongside in the sand. There were six or seven large flat stones that ran from the end of the porch out into the sand, apparently the remains of some sort of walkway. Overall, the beach house felt intimidating and mysterious. Seth, without realizing it, had already instinctively taken several steps back toward the water and away from the house. The look of the place alone was enough to strike fear into a man's heart, and Seth, though curious and anxious to find the meaning of his circumstance, was no different.

Keeping his eyes fixed on the eeriness in front of him, he began taking several steps backwards very quickly, until his foot sank a bit too far in the sand, causing him to fall backwards and land on his back with a thud. He gathered himself and stood. Instinctively, he began to call out for help in every direction.

"Hello?" He repeated this several times, but an answer never came. "Hello?" he screamed into the darkness. Nothing. "Is anyone out there?" His voice bounced off the beach house and echoed back to him.

Feeling scared and lost, he wondered if he even wanted an answer to come back out of the darkness. He could only imagine what that might bring with it. He was cold, naked, alone, and with the weight of his solitude now thrust ever stronger upon him, he looked once more at the beach house. It stood there half hidden in the darkness as if crouched and ready to attack. It stared back at him with a cold and stark look that made him shiver. Finally, the fear overwhelmed him and he did the only thing he could think to do... run.

Perhaps it was instinct and not thought that sent him into the darkness, but he turned his back on the beach house and ran along the edge of the water, away from his fears, away from his solitude, and towards anything else he could find. It didn't matter at this point where he went. He didn't care. Any place would do.

Any place but here...

He ran and ran, as long and as far as he could. His muscles strained as if this were the first time they had ever been called into action. At first he felt almost nothing as he ran. No burn in his muscles, no strain in his chest, no sweat on his brow. Silence and numbness engulfed him. The only thing that joined him in his flee was his fear, tagging along behind him and nipping at his heels like a ravenous wolf, urging him on more and more.

The darkness felt like a fog, uncovering as much before him as it hid behind him. Yet, as he ran, he saw only more sand and more water with each step. Every extra yard he could see in the darkness brought the same view as the last. Nothing new appeared on the horizon, nothing to his right or left, and he dared not look behind him. He simply ran, with the tenacity and vigor that only comes when motivated by an outside force so strong that you can find within you a strength you never knew you had. Seth was calling on this strength now, and to his best estimation, he had run for a full eight or ten minutes without finding anything along the way. Occasionally he would call out between his breaths for someone, anyone that might shed light on the darkness in this place, and in his mind. Yet, no one answered. The beach had remained the same.

With his head down, he stared at the sand before him. He watched each step, as they gradually became more tedious and more difficult. His sprint had slowed to a jog. His feet became heavier and heavier, and they started to drag the sand with each passing return to the front. He was breathing heavy, but with little reward. The air was weighty and fruitless, and each time he filled his lungs he seemed to acquire less and less oxygen. His steps slowed more and more until they stopped all together. He stood, hunched over, sucking in breath after heavy breath, and staring at the dimly lit sand below him, glowing from the moon above his back. He was exhausted. Unable to support his own body with his legs anymore, he fell to his knees and closed his eyes for a few moments to gather himself.

When he opened them and turned to look behind him, he saw an infinity of sand, marching off into the distant darkness, leading to nothing, to nowhere. He had made no progress.

Staring back along the path he had just run, trying to decide if he should continue, a startling revelation jolted him. From far off in the distance, leading up to his last step in the sand before him, something was missing.

No footprints!

Not one depression showed the path back the way he came. The sand was smooth and the surface was polished, as if untouched by anything or anyone for an eternity. It was as if he had not moved an inch since he arrived. If not for the orientation of the water, Seth would have no way of knowing which way he ran at all. It all looked the same to him. His hands began to tremble as a tear formed in each of his eyes. He looked down at his hands and pushed them deep into the sand in front of him. As he slowly lifted them and watched the sand fall back into place, there was no mark left behind. Fear knocked him backwards.

What is going on? Am I losing my mind?

He collapsed onto his back and let the feeling sweep over him. His thoughts ran in every direction. He looked up at the moon in the dark sky. It shined down on him like a spotlight, illuminating his solitude. He turned his head towards the water and scooped up another handful of sand, letting it fall between his fingers. His mind spun in circles trying to make sense of it all, and as he pondered the possibilities, both his thoughts and his body seemed to slip away from him. Still naked, still confused, he put his hands over his head, closed his eyes, and began to cry. Every ounce of him strained against itself for answers, but more tears were all that came. This world and all of its darkness pressed in on him, and weighed him down. His mind gave up. It did the only thing it could at this point. It shut off, and the body soon followed suit.

Seth passed out on his back in the sand, and in that split second before his eyes rolled back into their own dark world, he wondered, or more accurately... he hoped. *Maybe this is all a dream...*

CHAPTER TWO

STATION 119

8:22 p.m.
Sept. 6th, 2002
Sangamon County Fire Department
Springfield, IL

Charlie stood in front of the station. There was a faint red glow bouncing off his cheeks and his forehead from the neon lights in the sign above. The light bathed the entire front of the building along with the sidewalk below in the same shade of red. An American flag flapped in the wind to his left, and the metal clip on the rope smacked loudly against the pole, which drew his attention.

He looked up at the words "Sangamon County Fire Department." In smaller unlit lettering directly beneath those words it read "Station 119, established 1887." Charlie noticed the "e" in "Fire" was flickering on and off, making a slight buzzing sound that faded in and out with the light.

Seven months and they still haven't fixed that damn sign, he thought to himself, cracking a wry smile and shaking his head slightly. A part of him enjoyed the fact that the sign was still broken. It was this bit of consistency and stability that he needed in his life, yet had been unable to find since the accident.

Charlie pulled his cell phone from his pocket and stared at the backlit screen. He pressed a few buttons until he found what he was looking for, and then slowly put the phone to his ear, like he had done countless times in the last few months. "Hey dad, I was wondering…" After several seconds, he pulled the phone away from his ear before the words on the other end even finished. "…when I see ya." He closed the phone and put it back in his pocket, as a tear fell from his eye onto the pavement below.

He wiped his eyes and looked up into the night sky. He felt the mist on his face of a fast approaching rain, which would likely be here in minutes. A few drops had already landed on his face. Above, he could see the lights on upstairs through the second story windows, and could hear the faint din of the men upstairs. He had been gone from the station seven months and twelve days as of this morning, yet he knew that upstairs he would find the same exact scene as the day he last slid down the pole. The boys at station 119 were accustomed to quiet nights in Springfield, and spent many of these nights engaged in a "friendly" poker game that had no real beginning, and no real end. The guys came and went, and sat at the table whenever their shifts collided, and each fireman kept a spare hard hat on top of his locker filled with quarters, dimes, and nickels. On a lucky night, he might add a few dollars to his hat, ready and willing to give it all back the following night. A group of firemen is a close-knit group, and camaraderie was what they truly played for.

He wondered if his hard hat was still there, resting on the top of one of the lockers, gathering a slight film of dust, and holding the loot he'd won months ago.

Charlie made his way inside the main doors and stopped for a moment in front of the trucks. There were two of them parked side by side, just inside the giant garage doors that led to the street. The trucks were kept in pristine condition, and the men rotated regular maintenance duties to keep them that way. They treated the fire trucks like sacred objects within these walls, and as in most stations, the trucks were given names by the men. To Charlie's left was "Hell's Nightmare" and on his right was "Tidal Wave." He ran his hand along the front of the hood and along the curve over the wheel well. Charlie could see his reflection in the shiny chrome bumper. These last seven months felt like seven years to Charlie, and his face seemed to show it.

He peered up the long stairwell that led to the second floor. The sounds of the poker game beckoned him from upstairs.

"Dan, would you make a decision already!"

"I'm thinking! Why don't you just calm down a second!"

"Well, you picked a hell of a time in your life to start thinking!"

"Hey, Hal, if I'm not mistaken, you've lost more money tonight than anyone at the table, so maybe it wouldn't be a bad idea to do a little thinking yourself."

"Maybe it wouldn't be a bad idea if you shut the hell...."

The poker game and the ribbing came to an abrupt halt

when the guys heard the door creak open behind them. Charlie stood in the doorway, and when the guys noticed him, he immediately began grinning from ear to ear.

"Chuck, you old dog, glad to have you back!" Hal stood up with a wide grin on his face. His shoulders were broad from years of heavy lifting, and Charlie noticed his trademark limp.

Charlie stepped into the room with a much-needed smile returning to his face. "Glad to be back. I see you're still hobbling around on that old busted leg of yours, Hal."

Dan, tall and slender, with an air of arrogance around him, stepped forward to shake Charlie's hand. "Boss said you might be back this week on night shift, but we weren't too sure you'd come."

"I couldn't get your hopes up like that and then disappoint, now could I?"

Nick, smaller and more reserved than the rest of the guys, yet the hardest worker of the bunch, smiled and silently shook Charlie's hand before being interrupted by Hal. "Well, your stash is still above the locker. Have a seat. Deal him in, Nick."

Charlie looked at the name badge that still adorned his old locker. It read "Charles Hatfield" in bold box lettering. On a piece of beige masking tape on the hard hat, peeling slightly at the edges, was the handwritten name "Chuck", as he was affectionately known among the guys at the station.

"You boys been busy tonight?" Charlie asked as he opened his locker and hung his coat.

Nick began dealing the cards as Dan spoke up. "Not really, a minor accident on Jefferson and some loony burning trash off Dirksen that got out of control. But hey, at least we got out of here for awhile."

Charlie grabbed the hard hat and blew the dust off. "I

guess not much has changed. That's what I like about this place."

"I'm in," said Nick. "We weren't sure you'd ever come back Charlie. Takes a lot of guts to get back on the horse after getting bucked like you did."

Charlie took a seat, poured some change out in front of him, and sat his hard hat under his chair. "To be honest, I wasn't sure either. But I couldn't sit at home thinking about it anymore."

"I fold." said Dan. "So Charlie, what have you been doing the last seven months?"

Charlie tossed a quarter into the pot. "Well, I stayed up late drinking, slept most days, read a lot of books, and started writing. I guess mostly I just lost track of time. Suppose I needed that."

Dan ran his fingers through his pile of coins, jingling them as he always did, attempting to get under the skin of the others when he wasn't participating in a hand. "Hope you weren't too hard on yourself Chuck. There wasn't anything you could do. I mean, he would have been on that road that night whether you worked the late shift or not."

"Take it easy guys!" said Hal as he mucked his cards in the center of the table. "Charlie just got here! Would you give him a break? The man's first day back and all you want to do is make him relive it. And Dan, I swear if you don't stop messing with those coins…"

"It's okay, Hal. I've already tried ignoring my problems, and that didn't make them any better either. Being back here is the only thing I figure will get my head straight. Back here at the station, where things make sense." Charlie flipped over his cards. "I got the flush."

Nick looked over the hand and realized he was beat, yet again. "Well, I'll be damn, I guess one thing definitely hasn't

changed around here!" he said as he folded the losing hand.
Charlie began raking the pot with his trademark grin on his face when suddenly the scanner interrupted them.

"...That is affirmative... we are currently on North Veteran's Parkway between Browning Road and the I-55 Interchange... small passenger vehicle heading eastbound in the right lane lost control and went over the embankment near Pigeon Creek..."

Hal reached around behind him to the scanner resting on the table and turned up the volume. "Listen up, guys."

"No other vehicles were involved... spotted by channel 13 news helicopter... vehicle does not appear to be in the water... we'll be there in five minutes... requesting immediate ambulance and fire dispatch..."

Hal stood up and pushed his chair in. "That's us boys. Game's on hold for now. Nick, head downstairs and fire up Nightmare. Dan, sound the alarm and gear up." Then, with a concerned look on his face, and using a more solemn voice, he turned to Charlie. "Why don't you sit this one out, Chuck? Stay back at the station and keep an eye on things... get reacquainted and all."

Charlie opened his locker and grabbed his coat and boots. "I didn't come here to hide from things, Hal. I've been hiding for seven months."

"I understand, man. I just think maybe you should ease into it that's all, make sure you're up for it."

Charlie fastened his belt and began lacing his boots. "If I wasn't up for it, I wouldn't have come." The station's sirens began blaring. He heard the truck engine thundering below. He stood, walked past the table still full of cards and coins toward the pole, and with his back still facing Hal, he said, "See you on the truck." Hal grabbed his gear out of his locker, mumbled something under his breath while shaking his head, and then followed after Charlie down the pole.

As Charlie reached the first floor, the large main garage door was already on the way up. The headlights on Hell's Nightmare were blasting through the rain and glistening off the puddles forming on the sidewalks and the concrete drive. The four of them found their familiar places on the truck, and a mere two minutes after listening to the scanner, they were pulling out of the garage and on route to the accident.

Seven and a half minutes later, they approached a scene of lights on North Veteran's Parkway, somewhere on the loop around Springfield, past the outer edges of the city. Four police cars were all aimed in the same direction, their red and blue lights flashing, their spotlights aimed at the scene. As the firefighters approached, they caught bits and pieces of the police cars and officers in red and blue flashes. Hal pulled the truck over and as soon as it came to a stop he turned off the sirens. The guys hopped out and ran over to the deputy in charge of the scene.

Hal removed his hardhat and reached out his hand. "What do we got, officer?"

"Red Pontiac Grand Prix tore through the guard rail. Lost control on the wet pavement, I guess. Didn't reach the water though, got hung up on a tree. Ran the plates, belongs to a twenty-one-year-old male. No one's been down there yet, and we have no way of safely reaching the car. Don't know if he made it. That's why we called you boys in."

Hal began shouting orders. "Get behind the wheel, Dan! Nick, man the ladder! Officer, if you could have your men move that patrol car and clear out a little, we're gonna back the rig up to the rail, and lower the ladder down to the car."

As the men scattered and the engines fired up, Hal turned to Charlie. "Chuck, I'm your boss, but I'm not going to tell you what to do, although I think maybe you should hang back on this one."

Charlie said nothing, but turned with a look of determination on his face, walked back to the truck, and hopped up on the back with Nick. As they backed up to the guardrail, he climbed up onto the ladder, with a determined look on his face. "I'm going down there," he told Nick. "Get me close." Nick offered no rebuttal, but simply nodded. Charlie climbed out on his belly near the end of the ladder, and Nick began lowering it down to the car, as onlookers gathered on the sides of the road. The distance was perhaps twelve or thirteen feet beneath the level of the highway, and maybe a little less horizontally away from the road. Charlie was lowered at roughly forty-five degrees headfirst towards the rear of the car, which was facing away from him, and suspended nearly twenty feet from the water below. The car was still upright, but tilted a little down towards the water. The rain was still coming down, and the parts of the car that were not covered in debris were glistening in the spotlights. The license plate on the rear of the car read "PUCK 32."

Charlie called out. "Hello? Can you hear me?" There was no answer. He strained to see into the front seat, and although he could sense a presence, he could see only darkness and shadows. "I'm coming to get you, just hang tight."

As the ladder neared the car, Charlie yelled back to Nick. "That's close enough." The ladder kept coming though, as Nick could barely hear through the rain and sound of the hydraulics. "I said stop the ladder!" Charlie shouted. The ladder scraped the trunk of the car, putting grooves in the red paint before finally stopping, causing the car to shift slightly in the tree. Charlie closed his eyes and held his breath as the car teetered back and forth on the limbs, praying it would hang on. Luckily, the car was gripped too tightly by the limbs to fall with merely a bump, so Charlie's attention immediately turned to finding the driver, after a quick glance down at the water below. "Is anyone in there?" Charlie yelled through the sound of the pouring rain hitting the metal of the car. There was no answer. He climbed even further out on the ladder, slowly, as each movement by him caused the ladder to scrape the car even more. "Hello?" He screamed into the darkness inside the car through the rear window, which had been busted out.

    Then, amid the sound of the rain and wind in the trees, he heard a voice. He could not see the origin of it, nor could he make out any words, but he knew he had found what he was after. "There's someone inside the car!" he shouted back up to Nick, who relayed the message to the others. Charlie shined his flashlight into the car. The passenger door was open and he could see the water below through the opening. At first he could not see anyone, and then as his light passed over the driver's seat, he saw a hand, then a face. It was a boy, probably in his twenties. His shirt was torn and he had blood on his face and hands. He was facing Charlie, with his back against the driver's door and left side of the steering wheel. He had a stark look on his face, and his eyes held a blank stare.

    "Are you hurt?" Charlie shouted. "Can you move?"

    Without an answer or a change in his expression, the boy reached for the driver's headrest and tried to pull himself up, causing the car and tree to creak and moan. He froze his movements until the sounds stopped. "It's all right, I'm going to get you out of here." Charlie said, trying to comfort the boy, who was still a good five feet away from the ladder. "I need you to listen to me and keep your eyes focused on mine. Now move slowly and try to get to the back seat."

    As the boy inched towards the rear of the suspended car, Charlie crawled down the ladder trying to close the distance between them. He now had his entire upper body hanging off the ladder and reached his hands out for the boy. "You're almost here," he said in the most comforting voice he could manage.

The boy made it to the back seat and reached his hands and head out the back window towards Charlie. The rain pelted the boy's face, washing away some of the blood that was now dripping into his eyes. With the gap between the two now at only two feet, both sides reached and struggled against gravity and the rain to close it. Their hands finally met and Charlie held on as the boy inched out onto the trunk of the car. "I have you now, I won't let go." reassured Charlie. The car teetered back and forth on the tree as the boy crawled towards the ladder. Charlie slowly backed himself farther onto the ladder, as the boy got closer, never letting go of his hand. He continued to hold his hand as the boy crawled onto the ladder. Charlie shouted above. "He's on, get us out of here!"

Nick hit the switch to reverse the ladder and it began inching away from the car, screeching as it scraped the metal below. Once the ladder cleared the trunk and the weight of Charlie and the boy was freed, the car shifted and the tree creaked even louder. The car's position in the tree changed, compromised by the ladder, and the limb supporting it finally gave way. As the wind howled around them, a loud crack sounded, which even the guys up on the road could hear. The boy never flinched nor turned his head, but stared up at Charlie with that same blank expression. Shock, Charlie figured. He looked below and watched as the car fell the remaining twenty feet into the water. The men above all rushed to the edge to look down after hearing the loud crash. The car slowly sank. Charlie felt the weight of the boy against him. He had finally passed out. As they reached the top, Charlie handed the boy over to the paramedics, who wrapped him in blankets and placed him on a stretcher.

The others ran over to congratulate Charlie, but the words just washed away in the rain as Charlie stood, wearing his own blank expression, and watching the boy on the stretcher roll away. The whole scene seemed to melt around him into a blob of meaningless rustle and bustle, as his eyes never left their mark. The rain fell on Charlie's head and dripped in his eyes, but he never wiped them dry. The others spouted out question after question, and each went unanswered and unnoticed. They looked back at the boy being loaded into the ambulance and couldn't help but notice the resemblance of this scene to the one Charlie had faced a mere seven months ago. A silence seemed to fall on the group as they realized Charlie was reliving his son's accident. The rain, the police cars with their flickering lights, the ambulance, the paramedics and the stretcher, all seemed to resemble that day out of his past. Even the boy himself reminded the guys of Charlie's son. Hal stepped closer and put his hand on Charlie's shoulder. "You all right, buddy?"

Charlie didn't answer.

"Let's get out of here. You've done enough for your first day back."

"I'm going with him," Charlie said without taking his eyes off the boy, as he took a step towards the ambulance.

"You don't have to go. He's in good hands now. You did your part." Hal's words bounced off Charlie's back with no effect.

"Chuck!" shouted Dan through the rain. Charlie simply kept walking. "Chu.."

"Guys..." said Nick, cutting him off. "Let him go. Maybe he needs this." Nick turned and ran over to Charlie, stopping directly in front of him. Charlie's walk came to an abrupt halt and he looked at Nick with that same steely glare of determination. Nick simply smiled and said, "Take care,

Chuck. You know where we will be if you need us." He stepped aside to let Charlie go, and Charlie nodded to him as he passed, then walked up to the ambulance. "Got room for one more?" The driver nodded and Charlie hopped in the back. Nick walked back over to the other guys, who all turned to watch as the doors on the back of the ambulance shut with Charlie and the boy inside.

Nick shook his head. "Hope he finds whatever he's looking for."

The others nodded in agreement and watched the ambulance drive away.

CHAPTER THREE

THE DARK ABYSS

Seth awoke. There was no hesitation this time, as he immediately sat up and looked to his left and right. He was still on the dark beach. In both directions was an endless ribbon of sand against the water reaching out into the distance. He looked above him at the bright moon, then down at his figure. His naked body told him nothing had changed from the previous time he woke here on this beach. His skin was still pale and colorless, and the air was still cold and held a feeling of foreboding.

He turned around quickly when he remembered the reason for his fear and panic the night before. There stood the beach house, just as he remembered it, grinning back at him with that haunting stare. He felt pulled to it for some reason, yet at the same time, he wanted to run from it just as the night before. These two emotions raged within him like a war, fighting over which would control his next move. The blood in his veins began to accelerate, and he could feel the fight or flight reaction building in him from the adrenaline. The hairs on the back of his neck stood up, as if ready to run themselves.

He turned back to the water and walked over the edge where it met the sand. The line on the ground separating the sand from the water was very straight, as the water seemed to be stationary. Wondering why it appeared so much like oil, he bent down and examined the water closer. Nervous at first, like someone testing the temperature of a hot pan, he touched the water with his fingers and quickly pulled them out. The water was cold and smooth, and rolled off his fingers so quickly that it left no residue or dampness behind. He scooped some up in his hand and swirled it around a little. *Definitely water*, he thought, but somehow it felt different. *Nothing in this place is like it should be. Nothing seems real.*

He looked out over the water to the horizon to see if he could spot some land or a boat, but he could not see far into the darkness. The water faded into nothingness and there was no way of telling how far it spanned. He turned to take one more look at the beach house. *No way am I going in there.* Turning back towards endless water, he took a step forward until his toes touched the liquid. *What do I have to lose*, he thought, as he took another step. *I have to get out of here.* That was his only thought as he lost all care and began running out into the water. It seems fear had won the battle within him. Once the cold water reached his chest he began swimming with all his energy. It was thick and cold and each stroke was a struggle to keep his body above the surface.

After swimming for nearly ten minutes, his muscles forced him against his will to take a break. He slowed to a stationary paddle and slowly looked around. There was nothing but water in every direction. The beach was far behind him and he could no longer see it or the ominous beach house. Remembering the futility of his last escape attempt, a simple encouraging thought crossed his mind. *At least I'm making progress this time.* With this reassurance, he swam with even more vigor out towards the nothingness. Each time his head raised above the surface, the water just rolled off of him, leaving him dry. The sensation was eerie, but he ignored it, choosing to focus on his simple task at hand, to get as far away from the beach house as he could, and perhaps find a way to be rescued.

After another ten minutes he began to tire, and stopped a second time. After looking around, he still found himself alone, with nothing in sight. He stopped kicking to let himself slip under the surface of the water for a second, if only to rest his legs. He opened his eyes and saw no fish, no coral, no living creature of any kind. He wondered how long he could swim, but refused to let himself consider the consequences of what might happen if he found nothing out here and no one found him. Fearing he may have lost his direction, he rose to the surface and took a deep breath. He had spun several times while looking around, and wasn't sure exactly which direction he was heading. The air was heavy and rather empty. He looked above. The light of the moon offered no guidance as to what direction he was facing, or going, or came from, for it fell upon him from straight above. He was tiring fast, and knew that he could not keep this up much longer. He yelled out into the distance for anyone that might hear his voice. "Hello... is anyone out there? Hello..."

No one answered his repeated calls, and no echo came back to greet him. He was most definitely alone, and losing strength fast. To conserve energy he tried floating on his back, but the water seemed unable or unwilling to hold him. It seemed to be getting thicker and thicker and each minute that passed made it harder for him to keep his head above the surface. He was spinning in circles looking for something, anything to grab onto, when some water slipped into his mouth just as he was taking a breath. He coughed hard to expel the water, using most of his remaining energy, and panic began to set in. *What do I do now?*

His arms felt like iron poles in the water, and after a few minutes he could no longer hold himself up. He took one last giant breath and then sank slowly below the surface, still looking up at the moon. The light was bent as it passed through the water and it looked like the moon's edges were wavy, no longer forming a perfect circle. With nearly two feet of water above his head, he convulsed and shivered with fear. He let that last breath escape him and found the strength to pull one last time with all the power left in him. He thrust himself towards the surface, sticking his hands out as far as he could, trying to reach the cold air above for one last gasp. His mouth, inches from the surface, strained to reach it. His hands pierced the surface and felt the air, but not his mouth. His pull was not powerful enough and he began to sink again.

He could no longer move his arms. The weight of each of them was bringing him down. He was helpless, a heavy body sinking towards the dark abyss below him while his arms reached hopelessly for the ever-growing abyss above him. The moon seemed to shrink, as the water pressed in on him from all directions. His heart pounded and he could feel the pressure building in his chest and his eyes. His stomach jerked and his mouth opened, letting the water pour into his lungs. At first it burned, and it shook him violently. The cold pierced his core and he felt the iciness inside him. As cold as the air was, the water in his lungs seemed so much colder. He looked around, but direction was meaningless. The only direction that mattered was up. He felt tired and both heavy and weightless at the same time.

    At once his muscles relaxed. His panic faded along with everything else in his world. He no longer seemed to notice the cold. His heartbeat slowed almost to a stop, and his limbs lost their struggle. His fear escaped him much as his last breath did, and he wasn't scared anymore. Instead he pictured himself lying in a bed about to fall asleep. He closed his eyes and almost convinced himself the bed was real. Then he opened his eyes and looked above him, catching a glimpse of the moon twinkling through the water, just as it disappeared into nothingness above him. He closed his eyes and dreamt of the sun, just before the darkness and cold took him...

CHAPTER FOUR

NO HERO

9:22 p.m.
Sept. 6th, 2002
Liberum Medical Center
Springfield, IL

The ambulance sped up to the emergency doors at the hospital and stopped with a sudden jolt, almost rocking Charlie off his seat. The paramedic in the back with Charlie didn't seem to notice. He had done this a thousand times before and his work never stopped even as they waited for the doors to swing open. Two doctors from the hospital grabbed the stretcher near the boy's feet almost immediately after the doors opened and pulled it most of the way out of the back. The paramedic along with Charlie each manned a corner near the boy's head and lifted as the wheels popped down onto the pavement. The two doctors led the way as the paramedic walked hurriedly beside, speaking in rushed tones. Before Charlie even had time to readjust himself, he was left alone in the back of the ambulance. He was amazed at the quickness and sheer efficiency of each man's movements as they worked seamlessly together, like some sort of rehearsed ballet.

Charlie jumped out of the back and his feet splashed in a puddle before stepping onto the sidewalk, just as the paramedic returned and hopped up into the back. The doors slammed behind him, the engine fired, and the ambulance was gone as quickly as it came. Charlie hurried to catch the emergency room doctors guiding the stretcher through the two sets of automatic doors. The wheels buzzed as they passed over the horizontal strips in the breezeway. On the way through the doors Charlie saw the familiar writing on the glass that triggered flashes of running through these very doors seven months earlier. The "Liberum Medical Center" in downtown Springfield was not where he pictured he would end up when he left the house this morning.

As the stretcher rushed into the emergency room, another doctor and two nurses immediately pounced on the scene. Around the room, babies were crying, people were coughing and hacking, and everywhere there was bustle and movement. At no time did the stretcher make a stop on its way through multiple doors and down a maze of hallways. Hospital talk bounced off the walls all around Charlie.

"What do we have here?"

"Caucasian male, early twenties, automobile accident. Became unconscious shortly after being removed from the car. Unresponsive since that time."

"This is the man who pulled him from the vehicle," said one of the paramedics while motioning towards Charlie.

"You say he was conscious when you pulled him out?"

Charlie answered with a nervous voice. "His eyes were open and he seemed to understand me, but he didn't talk. Just stared at me with a blank expression on his face. Passed out before we even got him in the ambulance."

The doctor turned to the paramedic nearly before Charlie was finished. "What was found during the en-route physical examination?"

"Multiple abrasions, including arms, head, and chest. Broken rib, possible punctured lung. Concussion, likely severe head trauma. Pupils were dilated and unresponsive."

The doctor turned to one of the nurses. "Call down and have surgery prep room four readied. Get me a Ketamine Hydrochloride drip set up and an IV kit."

As they approached a large double door secured with a locking mechanism, the other nurse turned and stopped Charlie. "This is as far as you go. I will escort you to the waiting room and someone will be with you in a little while to ask you some questions and get your information." The doctor entered a code into an electronic panel that hung on the wall next to the door and as it opened, the boy was rushed through along with everyone but Charlie and the nurse.

No one seemed to notice Charlie's exit or even took his or her eyes off the boy, and the rapid exchange of information never missed a beat.

"Any idea how the head injury occurred?"

"Most likely from blunt force trauma caused by hitting the steering wheel or windshield as the car struck the tree. Also possible side impact with driver side window."

"We could have intracranial bleeding causing pressure on his brain. Did you notice any involuntary movement or contraction of the muscles on the ride here?"

"None that we noticed."

The doctors rushed the boy into surgery prep room four and wheeled him over to a table nearly the same height as the stretcher. The paramedics unstrapped the board and lifted it onto the table.

"Let's have a look at his wounds. Cut his clothes off."

A nurse stepped in with a large pair of scissors and cut his rain soaked shirt straight up the center and down both sleeves, exposing his chest and arms. She then cut his jeans vertically on each leg to expose his legs and removed his belt. Within thirty seconds the boy was on the table in his boxers. He had several bruises all over his body, and blood on his hands and face. The nurse immediately administered a needle to the top of the boy's hand and hooked up the IV drip. A heart rate sensor was placed on the tip of one of his fingers and connected to a large monitor next to the table.

The doctor gave his orders. "I want a full set of scans. X-Ray, CT, MRI. And get moving, we don't know how much time we have on this one."

#

Charlie stepped into the waiting room, a stark contrast from the hustle and bustle of the emergency room. After the door shut behind him, he stood there for a second, trying to process all that he had seen and done tonight. He was the only one in the room and it was so quiet that he could hear the hum of the soda machine sitting in the corner, and the rain bouncing off the windows on the other side. For the first time tonight he felt tired, and took a seat near the window. He hadn't done much physically in the last seven months, and he felt the adrenaline that was keeping him going pump excitedly through his veins. He glanced at a picture on the adjacent wall. It was some sort of inspirational poster, a picture of a beautiful country morning, with the sun rising over the water of a pristine lake. He read the words to himself.

> *Time can seem so far*
> *And the future ever vast*
> *But mornings quickly come*
> *And just as quickly pass*

Not just the mornings, he thought. *It all goes too fast.*

Piles of magazines were strewn about on the tables in between the chairs, and Charlie picked one up with an athlete on the cover to take his mind off of things. *Ten months old, huh? You would think they could afford new magazines.*

He tossed the magazine with last year's Super Bowl champion on the cover back onto the pile, and reached for his cell phone. He pulled it out, pressed a few buttons, and put it to his ear. After a few seconds, he snapped the phone shut and put it back in his pocket again. Just as he wiped the tear from his eye, a woman came in the room holding a clipboard.

"Hello, I'm nurse Pineida. Are you the fireman everyone's talking about, who pulled the boy from the car?"

"Yes, ma'am. My name is Charlie, but most folks just call me Chuck," Charlie said, as he fidgeted and pressed his right thumb into his left palm to ease the shaking.

She smiled. "Well, Chuck, I guess tonight makes you some sort of hero, huh? Do you happen to know the boy's name?"

"I'm no hero, ma'am. Anyone would have done the same in that situation, even you. Most folks would have. I don't know his name, but they are pulling the car from the water now. As soon as they get his information and belongings, I'm sure the police will try to contact his family. I think they are going to send his stuff here to the hospital for his family to hold on to."

"Well, I'll just need you to fill out this hospital form so we have a record of who came in with the boy, and then I suppose you are free to go. I'll be back in a bit to get it." She sat the clipboard on the seat next to him along with a pen and turned to leave.

"Excuse me ma'am, but I..." Charlie hesitated a bit before finishing. "If it's all the same to you, I'd like to stay until the family gets here. I would just hate to leave the boy alone at a time like this."

The nurse smiled. "Of course. I'll tell the doctors that you are staying and to keep you updated."

"Thanks." Charlie said, as he picked up the clipboard and the pen.

Nurse Pineida opened the door and turned to Charlie one last time. "You don't have to wear a mask and a cape to be a hero." She flashed a smile just before the door shut.

CHAPTER FIVE

DUSTY BOXES

Seth awoke. *I'm alive. But how could that be? I drowned. Did someone save me? Did the tide wash me back ashore after I went under?* The questions were mounting, and then he felt it. The sand. He was back on the beach. His body and hair were dry and there were no signs of being in the water at all. Was it real?

He sat up and looked around. Just as each time before, he was sitting in front of the beach house facing the water, with no clothes on, and no way out. He hung his head in defeat, beaten again in his attempt to escape this place. *Why can't I leave this place? Can't I even die here? Where the hell am I?*

He stood and turned around to look at the beach house. Several thoughts were running through his head while he tried to make some sense of things. He tried to use logic, since emotion was doing no good. *There must be a reason I can't escape this place. And there must be a reason I keep ending up right here in front of this shack.* Seth stared intently at the front of the beach house, as if trying to talk himself into something. *I guess there's only one way to find out.*

For the first time since he found himself on this beach, Seth actually took a step towards the beach house. It was a reluctant step, filled with skepticism and fear, but it brought him closer nonetheless. He walked slowly until he reached the stones leading out from the porch. None of them were complete anymore, and each lied together in pieces, like stone jigsaw puzzles. He tapped the first one with his toe, and carefully put some weight on it, as one might do on a frozen pond before committing to walking across it. The wood that formed the steps and porch was old and withered, and the steps seemed very brittle. With a creak accompanying each step, he slowly made his way up, as the steps had more strength than their appearance let on. Once he reached the porch he stopped and stood in front of the door. His curiosity seemed to be defeating his fear the closer he got to it.

He placed his hand on the railing that led around the porch, touching it if only to reassure himself that this place was real and tangible. The look of it, combined with the haze brought about by the moonlight and the darkness, reminded him of an old horror movie, or a bad dream. He stepped up to the broken window to the left of the door and tried to peer inside. Motionless shapes and shadows littered the floor, but what they were he could not tell from out here. He moved to the door, still hanging by a single hinge, and peered inside as best as he could. "Hello! Is anyone in there?" he shouted into the darkness beyond. There was no sound or echo coming back. It was as if the darkness simply absorbed the sound.

He reached down and grasped the handle. The metal

was cold in the palm of his hand. There was no need to turn it, being that the door was crooked and half disconnected. He simply pulled the door open a little, scraping it along the aged porch, scratching an arc into the wood as it went. The gap was now large enough so he could slip through if he turned sideways. He took one last look back at the water, looking for any excuse to change his mind. There was nothing.

He turned back towards the darkness that led into the beach house and took a small step through the threshold. *No turning back now.*

Once inside, he stood motionless and took in all that was before him, giving his eyes a few seconds to adjust. It was dark, lit dimly only by the moonlight that managed to find its way inside through cracks and crevices, or one of the many broken windows. The outside door he just entered led straight into the remains of what appeared to be a kitchen. Scarcely a single cabinet door had managed to stay attached, and the old fridge stood gaping open, also in want of a door, allowing him to see the emptiness inside. The entire house was mostly empty, long ago forsaken. A film of dust covered every inch of the place, and seemed to hang together as a solid mass in the air. With each step, he felt more and more dust touch the skin on his chest. Glass pieces glinted on the floor near the windows and broken splinters of wood lay here and there, at one time a part of a wall or a door or a ceiling. The very walls were crumbling, leaving dusty piles on the floor under them. Seth took each step with care, as the floorboards beneath his feet creaked, protesting his weight. This place was dead by any definition.

Seth walked through a little doorway to the next room, careful not to pierce his bare foot on some unseen misery. This was probably at one time a dining room of some kind. There was no furniture anywhere in the room, and the only thing other than the dust that occupied the floor was a collection of about twenty old cardboard boxes, stacked two high on one half of the room. From here he could see into the main room beyond, which was also mostly empty. He stepped past the boxes, through the arched opening in the wall into this room, and found a similar scene. Perhaps thirty or forty boxes, covered in dust, were strewn about here and there. *Was someone moving in? Or out? How long ago? Who were they?*

      He walked over to the stack of boxes and ran his hand across the top, brushing off an eight-inch thick layer of old dust that silently fell to the floor. In the path his hand just made, he could now read the words "Dishes" on the box, in faded black permanent marker. *Maybe one of these dusty boxes will have some clothes in it.* He brushed off another box. He saw a few letters scribbled in black ink, and continued wiping until the word "Books" was clearly visible. The box was not taped or bound shut, but the flaps were simply folded together, with one piece overlapping another. *Maybe there's a name inside one of these books,* he thought as he carefully separated the flaps. *Or an address...*

      When he opened the box, he picked up the book on top of the stack and dusted off the cover. Something about this book drew the attention of his eyes and mind. He smiled. *Great Expectations* by Charles Dickens. *One of my favorite books.* With book in hand, he walked over to one of the broken windows where the moonlight was at its brightest. Though he was still naked, his thoughts were focused solely on the book. He sat on the floor in the corner and leaned his back up against the wall under the window, letting the light from the moon shine over his shoulder. He opened the cover and the smell of an old book that hadn't been opened in a very long time engulfed him and brought an even bigger smile to his face. He always Loved that old book smell. Nothing was written on the inside, but he noticed that several pages were dog-eared on one corner. On each marked page, a small passage was highlighted, presumably the favorite passages of the book's former owner. He scanned the pages for a moment, silently reading to himself, before deciding to break the silence with his own voice.

"I Loved her simply because I found her irresistible… I Loved her against reason, against promise, against peace, against hope, against happiness, against all discouragement that could be..." He said the words aloud, his voice deep and haunting within the walls of the beach house. The loneliness of his voice reminded him of how truly alone he was in this place.

"It was impossible for me to separate her, in the past or in the present," he continued. "…from the innermost life of my life..." He was comforted by the sound of his voice giving life to the dead silence that hung around him. The simple act of reading about feelings that were so different from the ones he had inside himself in this place had a calming effect on Seth. Fear and Hopelessness were put on hold for a moment, and superficially replaced by Love. He flipped to another dog-eared page.

"Love her, Love her, Love her! If she favors you, Love her. If she wounds you, Love her." His eyes got heavy and weak. "If she tears your heart to pieces - and as it gets older and stronger, it will tear deeper - Love her, Love her, Love her!"

His breaths were longer and slower than they had been since he got here. The air seemed easier to breath, with more life in it than before, and he felt rested and relaxed for the first time.

He turned the page again and found another highlighted passage. "The air of inaccessibility which her beauty and her manner gave her, tormented me in the midst of my delight..."

He leaned his head up against the wall to his side, closing his eyes for just a second to rest them. Then he flipped to another marked page, and slowly and peacefully read the lines to himself in silence.

Pause you who read this, and think for a moment of the long chain of iron or gold, of thorns or flowers, that would never have bound you, but for the formation of the first link on one memorable day.

As he read the words, warming thoughts flowed through him like sweet red wine, and Seth closed his eyes and allowed himself to drift away into his mind, if only for a little while...

CHAPTER SIX

SOVANNAH

Seth was lying on his back when his senses drifted slowly back to him, blanketed in the warmth of the summer sun hanging in the sky high above. He felt below him and ran his fingers through the grass that leaned against his side. He had a look of surprise on his face. *Grass?* He opened his eyes and saw only blue as the sky above him was singularly colored, as if painted by the brush of an artist with only blue on his palette. The sun was alone in the sky, and in its four o'clock position, just managing to peak out from behind the large clock tower that rose high above the arboretum on campus.

Shaking off the slumber of an afternoon nap, Seth sat up and looked around him. He squinted and held his hand up in front of his face to shield the bright sun. His body was stiff and tired, apparently not ready to wake up just yet. A backpack that had been used for a pillow, along with some notebooks, pens, a textbook, and a novel were scattered around him in the grass. Seth put the notebooks and pens into his backpack and grabbed his textbook. *Journalism Basics.* He picked up the novel and looked at the cover. *Great Expectations* by Charles Dickens. Seth read the words and immediately remembered the beach house. *Wow, that was a vivid dream. Not sure what all that was about. The beach, the running, the drowning, the beach house, the boxes...* He shook his head and smiled to himself when he thought about it, chalking it up as another entry in a long list of odd dreams. Either way, he was glad to be back in college and free from the darkness. *I'll have to ask my psychology professor about that one.* He put the book in his backpack, stood up, and slung it over his shoulder.

On nice days, Seth and hundreds of other students would often spend what time they had between classes sitting out in the grass in the large arboretum reading a book, studying for their next class, or chatting with friends. The campus was very large, and many times it didn't make sense to go back to the dorms after each class. So everywhere you looked, you would see clusters of people walking or talking together or sitting under trees or near sidewalks, and some others that instead searched for quiet little nooks.

It was a perfect summer day on campus, and Seth was wearing his favorite khaki shorts. He looked down and noticed what shirt he was wearing. It was a blue T-shirt that often sparked questions from friends and fellow classmates. It read "Puck 3:2" --referencing a line from Shakespeare's A Midsummer Night's Dream, and made in the fashion of a common shirt worn by the Christians on campus that read "John 3:16."

The air was crisp, and it carried the familiar scents of

late summer - the grass, the trees that lined the walkways, the daylilies and lavender that decorated the entrances to several of the buildings. The colors were bright, and all around him he saw something else that reminded him how much he Loved the school here. There was a pond in the middle of the arboretum, protected on one side by a giant willow tree. This was a favorite spot for many of the artsy types on campus.

A long walkway leading to one of the beautiful limestone buildings was lined on each side by evergreen trees. Nearby a gazebo sat next to a little creek that wound its way through campus, and there were bridges here and there to get from one side of the water to the other. As a backdrop, the main library sat on a hill behind it all, overlooking what could be mistaken for a beautiful park, reminding everyone of the studious nature of his or her time here.

Remembering that his Journalism class started soon, Seth quickly looked down at his watch. He still had twenty minutes. *Plenty of time.* He passed by the beautiful campus art museum, remembering the words of his orientation tour guide from before his freshman year... "the entire building was built without using a single right angle, except where the walls meet the floors and ceilings, and even the steps leading..."

From here he passed by Woodburn Hall where he once accidentally pulled the fire alarm while another class was taking a test. He smiled at the thought and continued over to the walkway that followed the creek, known affectionately by the students as the "Jordan River." Being a mere eight feet across, "Jordan River" was a bit of an exaggeration, but the meaning that Seth attached to it made it seem endless. It represented more to him than just water winding through the campus, dodging trees and buildings and roads. To him it was a metaphor for the time that constantly trickled by in his life, slowly and steadily, with no hesitation. It was his future, flowing off into the distance. Obstacles in the water represented those in life, and bends in the stream mirrored the changes that we all have to go through during our time. It was this thinking that set Seth apart from the other students on campus. He saw things differently than most, with more depth. He spent long periods of time examining the small details of life, and was often caught staring at some tiny slice of nature with a look of wonder in his eyes. It was this wonder that amazed others, but only Seth knew the duality of what this extra sense brought to him. He could look at a stream and see the endless abyss of life, but at the same time, the blink of an eye in which it faded away.

Seth debated skipping class to spend the rest of the day walking around campus, simply examining its intricacies and absorbing the beauty of a late summer day. This was not an uncommon thing for him to do, and he often estimated (or bragged) that he attended roughly twenty-five percent of his classes and still maintained a 3.2 grade point average. He would also claim that one could learn a great deal more from the experience than from sitting in a class bored out of one's mind. The debate of what he would do on this day didn't last long. As he walked past the School of Journalism without breaking his stride, he thought, *It's just too nice outside to be cooped up in a room somewhere.*

As he walked, he watched the myriad of students diligently heading in every direction, and he wondered what they might be studying, or what plans for life they might have. He often wondered if they had all the answers yet, or at least thought they did, because he himself didn't really have any. All he had were ideas. *Journalism, business, teaching, photography, travelling, writing, poetry, experience, emotion...*

He walked around for nearly an hour just thinking, with no direction in mind, simply letting chance lead him wherever it might. He walked through the trails that led to the space observatory, nestled in one of the many wooded areas on campus. He passed Jordan Hall, the natural science building, where he once took a class about the life and biology of birds, to the mockery of his friends. The sunlit paths through the trees led him to the immense Student Union building, housing everything from a bowling alley to a clothing store. The building was so large, students often got lost in the maze of hallways and floors. Outside the union, students were throwing Frisbees and footballs, painting, reading, writing, and sitting in clusters studying.

      He sat on the outer steps of the west side of the union, people watching, when his eyes landed on a girl sitting all alone in the sun, reading a book. From where he sat he could barely make out the cover. He noticed she was reading the same book he was reading, *Great Expectations*. *Now that's my kind of girl,* he thought, as he tried to gather the courage to approach her. He watched as her long and flowing brunette hair blew slightly in the breeze, teasing him by hiding parts of her face from time to time, yet always landing perfectly where it belonged. She was thin and intelligent looking, with an intensity on her face as she looked down at the pages. Her skin was slightly pale, with a hint of pink from the summer sun. Her freckles formed little clusters on her cheeks, nose, and shoulders, and several ventured down her delicate arms.

      He took a few steps towards her, and then stopped to open his backpack. He pulled out his copy of the book and began fighting the nerves and fear building in him. She was one of the most beautiful girls he had ever seen, and his nervousness grew proportionately greater as the distance between them shrank. It didn't matter how strong or proud or bold he was in his mind. When he saw her, she captivated him, and time seemed to stop time for just a second. He couldn't take his eyes off of her.

When the last timid step was complete and he had finally reached her, he knelt beside her. Up close, she was even more beautiful than he could imagine. She looked intelligent, happy, and to Seth, somewhat angelic. She was wearing a little white sundress with black flowers on it, and a pink sash-like belt around her stomach.

"Hi," he said in a surprisingly confident tone. One word was all he could manage at this point. The lump in his throat prevented anything more. He simply smiled, expecting the worst.

She looked up at him and smiled back, easing his nerves a little. "Hi," she said. Her voice was soft and sweet, and her eyes were welcoming.

Seth held up his copy of the book. "I noticed you and I were reading the same book."

She carefully placed her bookmark in the book and closed it. "I guess you are right. I'm in W131, English Literature. Normally, I don't like book reports, but this book is really good actually. Are you taking that class too?"

Seth smiled and sat down across from her. "Actually, no, I'm not reading it for a class, it's just one of my favorites." He held out his hand. "My name is Seth by the way."

She reached out and carefully took it. "I'm Sovannah. Nice to meet you." Seth's heart leapt a little when their hands touched. Her skin was soft and warm and her hand felt so small in his. Her nails were painted red with little white flowers on each one, and he noticed the same white flowers on her toes, as they peeked out from under her. He tried not to hold her hand too long, as he looked into her eyes, but he lingered as long as he could, wishing he had the power to pause time for a while, to make this moment last. Her eyes were a brownish hazel color, so beautiful that Seth felt it was the first time he had ever seen this color before.

"Gorgeous day out, isn't it? I wish they were all like this," he said, without ever losing eye contact.

"I know. I could sit out here in the sun forever!" She placed her book on top of the others sitting beside her.

"Me too! Summer is definitely my favorite season." Seth looked up into the sky and smiled. He pointed above him. "In fact, that's one of my favorite phenomena. The sun and the moon are both out at the same time. I'm not sure why, but it always makes me smile." They both stared at the moon for a few seconds in silence before Seth spoke again. "So when's your next class?"

She looked down at her watch. "I have to be at Memorial Hall in thirty minutes. It's probably a twenty-minute walk from here. I was just about to leave. How about you?"

Seth stood, remembering how he was supposed to be in class at this very moment. "I'm actually all done with classes for the day, I was thinking about going for a drive later, but I have nothing until then. I could walk with you, if that's okay with you." He smiled, secretly holding his breath, waiting nervously for the reply.

"I'd like that," she said with an affirming smile on her face that nearly dropped Seth to his knees. She picked up her books and her pink cardigan and stood. "I usually take the shortcut down by the greenhouse over there. Ready to go?"

Seth finally took a breath. "Almost. What kind of gentleman would I be if I let you carry your own books?" Seth reached out and gently took the books from her. "Now I'm ready. Lead the way." As they walked side by side, Seth could barely hold back his excitement. Sovannah seemed sweet, honest, and smart. She was the most beautiful girl he had ever seen. And somehow she seemed to enjoy his company.

"Sovannah is a cute name by the way. How did you get

it? Is there a story there?"

"Actually, yes, there is," she said, as the sound of a few leaves crumpling accompanied their steps. "My grandmother had the name Sovereign, and my mother's name was Anna. She just combined the two and made a new name. That's why the second letter is an O. But a girl I met in one of my classes is from Cambodia and she said that my name means 'dream.'"

Seth kicked an acorn off the pathway. "Wow, dream, that's actually pretty cool."

"Yeah, I like it too." Sovannah followed suit and kicked an acorn too, smiling at him when hers went even farther than his.

Their hands accidentally bumped for a split second while they were walking, and in that brief moment, Seth thought he could feel the electricity exchanged between them. He wondered if she felt it too. "I'm not really sure what my name means."

"I like it. You should be glad it's only four letters. Try writing 'Sovannah' a hundred times a day for school, or filling in the bubble sheets for tests. It gets old." She looked over at him. "So Seth... what are you studying here?"

"Right now I'm studying journalism and business, but really I have no idea what I want to do. I'm not lucky enough to be one of these people walking around who have it all figured out." Sovannah seemed to be interested, so he continued. "There are lots of different career paths that have caught my attention at one time or another, but none ever truly felt like they were a good fit for me. I'm nearly done with my business degree and I realized something... I can't stand business. I hate it. It's not for me. There's no creativity, and I just don't want to end up with a dull and monotonous life, continually struggling to climb that corporate ladder. Bosses and cubicles, lunch hours and casual Fridays, time clocks and waiting for the weekend. The whole idea of it all just depresses me actually. That's why I started taking journalism classes. I suppose I always just assumed I would figure it out somewhere along the way. I don't know. I'm rambling.... How about you? Do you have it all figured out? What are you studying?"

Sovannah hesitated and cracked a smile. "Business... specifically Business Management."

Seth closed his eyes, pinched his lips together, and shook his head as his faced turned a shade of red that announced his embarrassment.

"Open mouth, insert foot. It's a talent of mine." They shared a small laugh together as they passed the large greenhouse on the south side of campus.

"No worries. I know it's not for everyone."

The sun was streaming through the glass of the greenhouse, and inside it looked like a tropical paradise. The windows were open and the smells of the plants inside saturated the air for hundreds of yards in every direction. Sovannah put her nose in the air. "Mmmmm. I Love coming this way this time of year." Seth nodded in agreement.

Despite his slam against the business school, she found herself somewhat drawn to his candor and willingness to open up. "My dad is a VP of Operations in Chicago, and my mom is an accountant there. I never really had a creative bone in my body, and I suppose business is just... in my blood. I wouldn't say I have it all figured out, but there's definitely a plan. What's your plan?"

Seth hesitated, not really sure how to answer. "Plan? I guess I don't really know at this point. I don't necessarily like the idea of planning everything. I sort of just want to see where life takes me. I mean, I used to have this detailed plan of becoming a rich computer guy, or a lawyer, with a fast car and a fancy house... but now I feel like I want more out of life than that... or at least something… different. I want to create something. I want to leave my mark. I suppose if I had to choose, I'd like to become a writer of some kind... maybe write the great American novel. Something that people would tell their friends about. Something that would linger with them long after they put the book down. Something that would make them think about their life, and see the world in a new way. I'd live somewhere amazing and I'd have this little room with a view... with shelves full of the great classics... *To Kill A Mockingbird... The Great Gatsby... Brave New World... The Catcher in the Rye... The Lord of the Flies...* and of course *Great Expectations.* I wouldn't need lots of money, either. I'd live humbly but I'd be wealthy in other ways. Does that sound crazy to you?"

Sovannah didn't answer immediately, as they walked up the front steps to Lindley Hall. She stopped on the stairs and turned to Seth. "Sounds great, actually. There are times when I wish I was more like you." She nodded towards the main doors a few steps up. "I suppose I should get in there and get some of this expensive education my dad is paying for. He always gives me a hard time if I miss a class. It was really nice talking to you though." She flashed a smile and slowly stepped up the last few steps. Reaching the door, she opened it in slow motion, almost as if she was waiting for something.

"Sovannah!" Seth shouted just before she escaped his view. His heart was racing with nervous excitement. When she turned around and looked back at him, he continued. "If you aren't busy after class... do you maybe want to... get some ice cream or something? My treat." The words were out there. He couldn't take them back. He felt triumphant just for asking, but now waited the grueling couple of seconds for her reply.

"I'd like that," she said with a smile.

"Okay. Let's meet outside the student union building. What time?"

"How about eight?"

"Sure. I can't wait." Sovannah slipped inside the doors and out of view, and Seth had to restrain himself from jumping up and down and pumping his fists like a wild man. Suddenly the sun seemed brighter to him, and the sky clearer. He walked with pep in his step that grew the more he thought about her. He continued on his walk around campus, with a smile that was etched on his face. He couldn't have removed it even if he wanted to.

Outside Ballantine Hall, he stopped to take in the scenery, as he had done a thousand times before, yet today everything seemed perfect. The trees were full of life, as birds and squirrels were abundant here. They figured out a long time ago that students tend to drop all kinds of food on their daily commute to class, and by just hanging around, they would eventually get a snack. Some students even brought food specifically for the birds and squirrels on occasion, and stopped to feed them on their way. Popcorn was a favorite of nearly all species it seemed.

The sun was shining down on Seth through the trees and as he walked he looked at the streaks of sunlight pouring down between the leaves above, examining the patterns of light that spread before him on the sidewalks and grass. He stepped into a large sunlit section, stopped, turned his face to the sun, and closed his eyes. He raised his head and felt the warmth on his eyelids, as he spread his arms wide. To a passerby, it might have looked peculiar, but Seth would never have noticed or cared whose eyes were on him. He simply lost himself in the moment trying to soak it all in. A squirrel quickly crossed his path, completely comfortable with all the people that constantly roamed around here. After picking up a nut, it scurried off to join its friends in the grass, as Seth stood there with his eyes closed to the sun, and his arms spread out wide, like a triumphant statue, thinking of Sovannah.

He opened his eyes and everywhere he looked he saw couples. Nothing changed in the mass of people teeming to and from the classes, but now he couldn't help but notice them all. It was his perspective that changed. A couple holding hands over here, or a young man and woman flirting over there, boys carrying books for girls. He was lost in himself when he woke up in the arboretum, but now he found himself lost in thoughts of Sovannah. Her beauty, her sweet voice, her soft skin, her intelligence, her innocence... all captivated his every thought.

He headed past the familiar buildings of Maxwell and Kirkwood, where he remembered sitting through lectures not paying attention. Instead he wrote poetry in his notebook, or stared out the window at the giant old magnolia tree blowing in the breeze, as the professor tirelessly talked of tangents and sine curves. He looked up and could remember the exact window next to which he always sat with pen in hand and mind afar...

Wake me up and show me how
To hang the moments on the bough...

He used to watch the birds play and dart through the branches. Occasionally one would land on the ledge just outside the window and mockingly stare at him inside his cage. It was as if the birds were asking him to come outside and play in the sun.

*Floating through this life with pride
On wings of freedom I shall glide
With skies so endless and so bright
I'll always be a bird in flight...*

He walked the trails that led through Dunn woods, stopping here and there to inspect some minute detail of the campus. Seth was the type of person that could spend minutes, or "waste" them as his friends would often say, watching an ant struggle up a tree, or holding a leaf up to the sun to inspect the veins, or watching two squirrels chase each other from one branch to another, wondering what they were thinking. It was one of the main reasons he chose to attend this school. The campus covered a few square miles, and contained woods, creeks, and endless walking trails that seamlessly blended into the surrounding natural fauna. There was something amazing everywhere he turned.

Seth made it to the student union building just before 8:00. The sun was nearly gone and the outside lights that lit the walkways would soon be on. After realizing how large of a place they chose as a meeting point, he wondered exactly which of the over twenty different entrances Sovannah would mostly likely be at. He decided to sit and wait by the most likely door based on the direction she would be coming from, angry at himself for his oversight. *Bookstore! Why didn't I say the bookstore entrance?*

Ten minutes after eight, Seth began to worry if maybe he had chosen the wrong door, and if she might be waiting for him on the other side of the building. He quickly ran up the steps and through the maze of hallways leading to the door on the opposite side, near the student commons. He looked around and couldn't find her there either. *It's almost 8:20, maybe she's not coming after all...* He sat down and waited until 8:30 before reluctantly deciding to head back to his room. His smile had left him. By now the sunlight was gone and the lights that lined the myriad of walkways around campus were all on. Seth turned his back on the union building and hung his head. Everything seemed quiet and dull, until something broke the silence.

"Seth!" He turned around. Sovannah was walking down the steps after him. The sight of her put a smile immediately back on his face. Though it was getting darker, when he saw her she seemed to light up the surroundings. "Sorry I'm a little late, I went to drop off my books in my room before heading over here so I didn't have to carry them around. Have you been waiting long?"

"Actually, I thought maybe you weren't coming."

She flashed a big smile back at him. "I wouldn't miss out on free ice cream! Don't think I forgot your promise… plus, I've been wondering all class what 'Puck 3:2' means on your shirt. I was distracted with it all lecture. So I had to come back to find out."

"So I guess I can thank my shirt for luring you back here? Perhaps I shouldn't tell you then, so you can't leave. You will have to keep seeing me until I finally tell you." They both shared a sarcastic laugh before Seth gave in to her request. "It references a line from one of Shakespeare's plays: A Midsummer Night's Dream. There is this fairy named Puck who watches the humans fall in and out of Love and generally make fools of themselves. While watching them, Puck says to himself: 'What Fools These Mortals Be.'" That line is in act three, scene two. He smiled as he watched her eyes staring back at him, full of eagerness and interest. "So now you know what it means. I guess you are free to leave now."

Sovannah smiled coyly. "I can't leave before ice cream, now can I?"

"I was hoping you'd say that." Seth led the way as they walked through the campus gates that graced the front of most of the University brochures, and over to nearby Kirkwood Avenue, which was lined on both sides with shops and bars, a bustling hotspot for student night life. They arrived at a quaint little ice cream shop called Soma. After ordering, they took their cold treats and sat outside in the little patio area, overlooking the street.

"Every time I come here I think of the book *Brave New World*," Seth said between spoonfuls.

Sovannah had a puzzled look on her face. "And why is that?"

Seth seemed amazed. "You don't get the reference?"

"No." Sovannah shrugged and bent her lips.

Seth burst out. "Have you never read it? Oh my gosh, you *have* to read it! It's my all-time favorite book! I'll even let you borrow mine if I have to. We have to remedy this situation."

She laughed at his intensity. "So why does this place remind you of that book exactly?"

"Well, the book is set in the future in a time when everyone is controlled by the government and not allowed to have true emotions. They all take this drug to keep them *happy* (Seth made little quotation marks in the air with his fingers) and under control, and the drug is called Soma. They have all these sayings about it. *A gramme is better than a damn...* Anyways, it's a book about Love and happiness and control and freedom and... you should read it."

She smiled and seemed to like his passion for things. She finished her last bite of ice cream and tossed her cup into the trash. "Thanks for the ice cream, it was yummy!"

They walked back to the arboretum, which was nearly empty now that it was dark out, mostly talking about books and movies. He took her over to the little gazebo outside the main library. Leading up to it was a little stream landscaped perfectly with rocks that created several tiny little waterfalls, and gave the night air a wonderfully relaxing background music of bubbling water. He held her hand as they walked across the slippery rocks, just as a frog leapt off the bank into the water near Sovannah. She gave a little girlish yelp, as if she had seen a mouse, which Seth thought was adorable.

When they stepped onto the other bank, Seth smiled and gave her a hard time. "Afraid of frogs are we? One of those could be your prince you know. Maybe I'll fish him out the water so you can give him a little kiss..." He jokingly reached his hand towards the water.

She giggled and smacked him on the arm. "You better not. I'll push you in."

"Alright, you win. But only because I just met you." Seth smiled and took her hand again. He was drawn to her like a strong magnet, and with each touch of her skin he felt the electricity between them grow. They sat on the grass in front of the gazebo. It was still warm from a full day in the sun. They laid on their backs and looked up at the stars and the moon.

"You know, when I was a kid I used to think that everyone saw something different when they looked up at the stars. Like when I looked up, I saw my stars, and when you looked up you saw yours. We all had our own stars. And every time we had a dream, a new star would get added to our sky."

"That's really cute." Sovannah smiled and looked at Seth, as he was staring above at the sky.

"I used to wake up after a good dream when I was a boy and run to the window to look up at the night sky and try to find my new star. Seems silly now, but back then it seemed so important and so amazing." Seth pointed above him. "That one over there is called Aquila. It means Eagle."

Sovannah squinted. "I'm not sure I see anything. Just seems like a jumbled mess of dots to me."

Seth leaned in closer to her. "See how those four stars form a large diamond? That is supposed to be the eagle's wings and body. And the single star down there at the bottom, that's the tail."

"Oh wait, I see it now. It looks like a kite." She smiled like a child in wonder. "Do you know any more of them?"

"Sure." Seth was happy to share what he knew and got excited when talking about natural wonders. "Right over there is Sagittarius. It's a lot harder to see. I just know that the line of stars on the right are supposed to be the arm holding the bow, since Sagittarius means archer."

"It's pretty." Sovannah stared above in awe of the stars, but also reserved some for Seth. He felt her squeeze his hand as he talked. Somehow, he managed to grow up and still hang on to his childlike wonder, and he could tell this impressed her. She pressed in closer to him. "I wish I knew more about this kind of stuff. My brain is filled with business models and legal statutes. I feel like such a grown up. Like I'm boring or something, compared to you."

Seth turned his head to face her and said jokingly, but with a straight face "I *DO* feel a little bored actually. Maybe I should go..." She playfully smacked him on the arm again and they both erupted in laughter, all alone on their backs in the arboretum, under the stars on a warm late summer evening. After the laughter tapered off, Seth looked at her again.

"Seriously though... you aren't boring. You're anything BUT boring. To me, everything seems a little better just because I'm with you. I'm really glad I bumped into you today. Tonight has been nearly perfect. Like a dream... I guess your name is perfect."

They stared into each other's eyes, and the look on her face told Seth all he needed to know. He slowly leaned in and their lips touched ever so softly. Waves of emotion surged through his veins, and he felt more alive than he's ever felt. He touched the side of her face with his hand and kissed her again. Her lips were soft and sweet, and felt warm pressed against his. The world could have ended right then and he would have barely noticed... or cared. He smiled and looked into her eyes, losing himself in their color again. "Okay, now it's been a perfect night."

She slowly smiled and Seth rolled to his back and looked up at the stars again. He squeezed her hand, closed his eyes for a while, and savored the moment...

CHAPTER SEVEN

LITTERED PAGES

9:22 p.m.
Sept. 6th, 2002
Liberum Medical Center
Springfield, IL

"Doctor Brigham to ER Consult Six." The Hospital intercom system blasted loudly through the halls of the hospital. "Doctor Brigham to ER Consult Six, STAT!" Charlie heard the announcement from the waiting room, wondering if it had something to do with the boy he pulled from the car. He could only lean his head against the waiting room wall and wait for answers.

Outside, the halls were abuzz, and down in ER Consult Room Six the nurse was waiting for Doctor Brigham to arrive.

The boy was on a stretcher in the room, unaware of the rustle and bustle of the many hospital technicians striving to keep him alive. On the wall the light board was fired up, casting a faint and ominous glow on everything in the room. On the table next to it lay several folders, containing the results of the boy's X-rays. The nurse anxiously watched the door.

"What do we have here?" the voice of the doctor was almost simultaneous with the sound of the door swinging open. He wasted no time.

The nurse handed him a folder. "Here are his X-ray results. There are fractures to the 4th thoracic rib, the left clavicle, and also the left first rib."

The doctor removed the plastic sheets and quickly snapped the first one onto the light board. He scanned the image quickly, and spoke to the nurse while his eyes never left the light board. "There may also be damage to the brachial plexus or the subclavian vessels, but neither of these injuries is life threatening."

He grabbed the second sheet and quickly stuck it on the light board as the nurse briefed him. "I'm afraid he also has a compound depressed skull fracture of the cranium just above the joining of the frontal and temporal lobes on the left side."

The doctor's expression changed immediately to one of concern and disappointment. "I was afraid of that. Have you done a CT scan?"

"Yes, I ordered it immediately when I saw the X-rays. He was taken in right away and just arrived back here a few minutes ago. The radiologist just called and is on her..."

Before the nurse could finish her sentence, the door burst open and a tall elegant woman handed the doctor another folder. She walked with a purpose and commanded attention wherever she went. The doctor grabbed the folder and quickly opened it to examine the photographs while the nurse and the radiologist stood in silence. They could tell by his expression the news was not what they had hoped.

"Yep, just what I feared. The depression of the skull has increased the pressure on the frontal lobe and there appears to be some damage to the soft tissues underneath. There is evidence of cerebral intracranial hemorrhaging. We need to go in immediately to relieve the pressure and remove the skull fragments or he's not going to make it. Get him down to prep room four now." With more urgency, he raised his voice, unhappy with the speed at which the staff moved. "The boy has minutes, not hours people. Get moving." The nurse immediately wheeled the stretcher out of the room as the doctor picked up the phone.

The voice on the other end was abrupt. "ER Surgery."

"This is Dr. Brigham, I have a young man, early twenties. Immediate response surgery required to relieve pressure on the frontal lobe. He is headed to Prep Room Four now. He'll need a ketamine hydrochloride drip ready to be administered there. Who is the on-call surgeon tonight?"

"Dr. Meeker. I'll send him to surgery prep now."

"Ok, I'm sending the scans his way." He handed the folder to the radiologist and she darted out the door. "I have to check in on a chemical burn in ER three, then I'll be down." The phone was slammed back in place and the room was empty in seconds.

#

Back in the waiting room, Charlie was flipping through the channels on the small television mounted near the ceiling in the corner, when nurse Pineida opened the door.

"Charlie, could you follow me, please."

Charlie grabbed the clipboard and pen and walked to

the door. "Here are the forms. All done."

She smiled as he handed them to her. "Thanks, Charlie. I'll send them to reception to get logged into the system."

They stepped outside the door to the hallway where another nurse, probably in her early twenties, waited. Her scrubs fit snugly to her body and hugged her youthful curves. They were a lively color of pink with a mesmerizing pattern of little puppy feet that ran all over her body. "This is Ramona, and she will be taking you down to the ER's main entrance. The police have arrived and are requesting to speak with you." Charlie simply nodded in agreement. "When you get back here, hopefully I'll have an update for you on the boy's condition."

"Thanks, I really appreciate it," said Charlie as he followed the young nurse's curves and puppy feet down the hall. After a series of turns and doors, they arrived at the main ER entrance, and Charlie saw the two officers standing by the front desk in full uniforms. One of them was holding a cardboard box, and the nurse simply stopped and nodded in their direction. Charlie walked over to them with nervous feet. He hadn't been in a situation like this for quite some time.

"Hello, officer, I'm Charles Hatfield." Charlie rarely referred to himself as Charles, but always seemed to use that name when addressing an authority figure. He reached out and shook hands with the first man.

"The car was pulled from the water at the scene about thirty minutes ago. Currently there is a team dredging the river bottom now."

Charlie had a puzzled look on his face. "Why would they be looking there?"

"Investigators on the scene have questions as to whether or not someone else may have been in the car with him at the time of the accident. They probably won't find anything, but it's standard procedure in a case like this. Anyway, we brought the boy's personal belongings that were recovered from the car." Charlie looked down at the box as the officer continued. "The family hasn't arrived yet, and we were told you planned on staying until they get here. I thought I'd see if you mind hanging on to it until then."

"Sure, that would be no problem at all." Charlie barely got the words out of his mouth before the second officer forcefully handed him the box, which hit his chest with a thud. Apparently the officers were ready to get home and get out of their wet uniforms. The rain had been pretty steady all day. The cardboard was damp and the bottom and sides of the box bent a little as he held it.

"We ran the plates and contacted the boy's parents. They were informed of the situation and were told where he had been taken. They were an hour away when we spoke and are headed here now. Suppose they'll be here by ten."

"Alright, thanks for the update. I'll take care of it for them until they get here."

"Thanks for your assistance." Charlie nodded and held the box as the two men turned and walked out the ER doors. He realized that he was all the boy had until the family arrived.

He turned and saw the young nurse across the room, waiting by the hallway. She smiled at him as he walked over. Once again, he eyed the nurse's curves and puppy dog feet scrubs as she led him back through the many hospital corridors to the waiting room. The room was still empty when he arrived, and the sounds of the rain and vending machine were joined by the faint sounds of the television that he had left on just minutes ago. He sat down, put the box in the chair next to him, and grabbed the remote to turn off the TV. All he wanted was a little quiet to gather his thoughts. He closed his lids to give his eyes a brief rest, just before the door opened again and nurse Pineida walked over to him.

"Hey, Charlie." Slightly startled, his eyes quickly opened. "You sleeping?"

"No, although I think I could use a nap. Have you heard anything yet?"

"I spoke to Dr. Brigham and I'm afraid he had some bad news for me."

Charlie's wasn't much for hiding his feelings. He put his hand over his mouth and his eyes opened wide, awaiting the news. The words came out nervously. "How bad is it?"

"The boy's skull is cracked, and they found some bleeding in his brain. I'm afraid they had to rush him to surgery."

Charlie hung his head. "He was awake when I pulled him from the car, but went unconscious pretty quickly. I'd say maybe eighteen to twenty minutes after the accident."

"I suppose that makes sense. Bleeding takes time. People often show no signs of serious head injury until hours after an accident."

"Poor kid." Charlie's eyes began to water a bit.

"Don't you worry, we have the best doctors in the country here. They will do everything they can." The nurse patted Charlie on the shoulder before leaving. "I'll keep you updated," she said as she walked out the door. She was impressed by how much emotion he had over a stranger.

Charlie looked at the floor and shook his head slowly. He said a little prayer to himself under his breath. His eyes closed and he wondered why this had to happen on his first day back at the station. *Now is as good a time as any I suppose.*

It was in this very hospital seven months ago, when Charlie's own son was all alone in a coma, about to take his last breath. He knew that nothing could ever make up for the fact that he wasn't there for Michael, but something inside him told him he needed to be here tonight, even though he knew little about the boy.

    Charlie opened the box next to him out of curiosity, perhaps to learn a little more about him, and perhaps just to pass the time. He read the titles of the textbooks to himself. *Business Law, Economics, Journalism Basics, American Literature. Smart kid.* There were several different colored pens, some loose change, golf balls, and a few CDs. One of the albums had a picture of someone shouting in pain, covering their face. *Third Eye Blind?* Another had a photo of a man basically doing the same. *Pearl Jam?* He flipped through the CDs, amusing himself with the names of the bands and the pictures on the album covers. *Linkin' Park? Our Lady Peace? Alice in Chains? Matchbox Twenty? Fuel? Live? Bare Naked Ladies?* Charlie hadn't heard of a single one of the bands before. *Guess I'm getting old.*

    There was a novel with several dog-eared corners under the other books. A metal bookmark was still stuck between two pages near the end of the book. Charlie opened the book to the marked page, noticing several highlighted passages, and read the laser-etched inscription on the bookmark. *Go Confidently in the Direction of Your Dreams... Live the Life You've Always Imagined... Henry David Thoreau.* Charlie stared at the words for a few seconds. *Good advice I guess.* He knew at his age he didn't have many dreams left. He lost them somewhere along the way in life. Now his sense of direction seemed amiss. He shut the book and set it aside, wondering what dreams the boy might have, hopeful one day they will become a reality.

    At the bottom of the box was an old beat up journal. Charlie pulled it out and flipped through several of the pages, which were still somewhat wet and stuck together in places. It was filled the boy's writing. Poetry, quotes, essays, thoughts, and a few drawings here and there littered the pages. Mesmerized, he read page after page until nearly forty minutes had passed. The boy's words were deep and powerful, and Charlie could feel the sincerity behind them. He flipped the pages ever so carefully, trying to understand the depth of the boy's thoughts. He eventually stopped to look at his watch. *The family should be here in fifteen minutes or so,* he thought, as he set the box with the rest of the boy's stuff aside. He crossed his leg and leaned back to read a few more of the poems, as the sounds of the waiting room remained the same. The vending machine to his left hummed and the rain bounced off the windows to his right. He pulled out his cell phone and set it on his lap, gripping it tightly.

CHAPTER EIGHT

SUBLIME PICTURE

Seth opened his eyes and stared at the stars above him. The sky was dark and the stars seemed to stand out more than usual. "Maybe I can find Orion's Belt. I always have trouble seeing Orion. I guess this might not even be the right time of the year for it. I can't remember..." He cupped his hands around his eyes and scanned the sky. "You've at least heard of the big dipper, right?" Seth said it with a hint of sarcasm, and waited for Sovannah's witty comeback, perhaps accompanied by a playful smack on his arm that she was accustomed to giving. Nothing came. "Sovannah?" He turned to see if she had fallen asleep in the grass. She was gone. Startled, he sat up quickly to look around.

"Sovan..." He started to call her name, but stopped abruptly when he realized where he was. He was no longer in college on the soft grass of the arboretum. His mouth was open and his eyes were wide, as he saw what was before him. *No...*

He was back on the dark beach, sitting in the sand, this time facing the menacing beach house, tattered and torn, just like before. His demeanor instantly changed, and his heart sank in his chest. The weight of the dark sky pressed down on him again. He looked up and saw the stars of the constellation Sagittarius, still hanging in the night sky, sharing it with the brightly lit moon. *Was it all a dream? Was Sovannah real?*

He sat and thought about Sovannah, and how they were lying on their backs looking up at the stars. It was as if he blinked and she was gone. He remembered holding her hand, and how soft her skin felt when it touched his own. The electricity flowed between them and up and down his spine. He sighed as he thought about the kiss they shared on that warm summer night, and the stark contrast to the bitter cold of this beach. He remembered closing his eyes in the grass and thinking it was the best moment of his life so far, and how lucky he was to bump into such an amazing girl outside the student union building. He thought about how beautiful and peaceful she looked sitting all alone in the sun, as countless students bustled by. She was in her own little world, and when he saw her, he was in her world too. She was the breeze in his hair, the warmth on his skin, and the sunlight in his darkness. He remembered how her hair swayed in the breeze as she looked down at her book.

The book! Suddenly Seth remembered going inside the beach house and finding the book in one of the dirty old boxes. The memory of the last time he was here rushed upon him like a wave. *I was by the window and was reading when I...* He stood up in a rush and stepped towards the beach house. There was no hesitation this time. He stepped on the unbroken stones leading up to the porch and hopped up on the weathered wood. There was an extra spring in his step this time, and he wasn't nearly as afraid as before, even though the beach house hadn't changed its foreboding appearance. *Where am I? What is this place?* He knew the answers must be inside.

When he stepped to the door, he saw something out of the corner of his eye that stopped him in his tracks. In a piece of broken glass hanging in the window, he noticed his reflection. He was no longer naked. He stepped closer to the glass to peer at his reflection. He was wearing khaki shorts and a blue t-shirt. He looked down and read the words. *Puck 3:2.*

The door was still pulled back from the last time he entered, and he slipped through the small gap into the darkness of the house. He was standing in the kitchen again and he looked around at the ruins. He saw one cabinet whose door had managed to avoid falling to the floor, and out of curiosity, he reached for it. As soon as he touched it, it fell with a crash onto the floor and dust poured out after it. *Good thing I'm not hungry.* He still hadn't lost his sense of humor.

He stepped through the dining room into the main living room and saw some of the boxes that he had rifled through the last time he was in here. The hand swipes that cleared the dust on several boxes still showed the words below. *Kitchen, Dishes, Shoes.* The box marked "Books" seemed to be gone.

Over by the window, the book he pulled from the box the last time he was here was still lying on the floor. He walked over and picked it up, flipping the pages as he thought about Sovannah again. He could see the marks on the floor where he sat in the dust reading. *I was sitting right there...naked. And now...* Seth had more questions with no answers. His logic tried to make sense of it all. *Did I find some clothes in another box? But then what? How did I get back outside? Why can't I remember?*

    Seth gazed around with a puzzled look on his face. He stood there looking off into the darkness, hoping the answers would just come to him. Adjacent to the largest room, presumably the living room, there was a hallway that led to Seth's left, running parallel to the beach. He walked over to it and peered down the hall. It was dark, but he could see light swatches on the broken floor boards at intervals down the hall, from the moon casting a glow through the windows in the rooms on the left. From these he could tell that there were two smaller rooms on the left, and another room on the right, along with the dusty remnants of an old bathroom a little farther down. At the far end, there appeared to be an opening to a larger room. *Probably the master bedroom.* It seemed to fade away in the distance and get lost in the darkness.

    He took a few steps down the hall and peeked into the first room on the left. He reached his hand slowly inside the door and felt along the wall for a light switch. When his hands felt it, it was already flipped up. He toggled it back and forth, but nothing happened, just as Seth expected. *Figures.* The room was dark, but the moonlight streamed in, casting a faint glow all across the room. A large bay window overlooked the water and the sand, which Seth didn't remember seeing from the outside. An easel about five feet tall was standing just off to the side. It had three legs and was made of wood that over the years had splintered and peeled. The canvas fell off years ago and was lying on the floor just below it under nearly half an inch of dust and dirt. *Whoever lived here was a painter.* Seth realized that any piece of the puzzle would help him figure out where he was.

    He took a few steps into the room, as the boards creaked under his weight. Several other blank canvases leaned up against the wall near the window. Old glass jars of paint were scattered everywhere, with a large collection of them gathered on the ledge of the bay window. Some of the jars were broken, while others were tipped over. To Seth's eyes, they were all various shades of black and gray, but he imagined they must have been brilliant colors at one time. One jar had several brushes of varying shapes and sizes sticking out of it. He looked all around the room at the individual paintings strewn about. A few were in frames affixed to the walls, depicting various beach scenes, but most were lying in stacks or leaning against the chairs and walls. Something about the room made Seth smile. He was always impressed by those who could paint, and part of him always wished he had the talent, but it was something that he just could never do. Several attempts of his had ended in messy disasters, and that was all the confirmation he needed. He stepped towards the door to the hall, accidentally kicking over a jar on the way by. Out of habit, he flicked the light switch on the wall to the "OFF" position on his way out, though it made no difference.

    A few more steps down the hall towards the second swatch of light on the floorboards brought him to the next room on the left. It was exactly the same shape and size as the first room, with an identical bay window overlooking the water and the sand. *This shack is bigger than it appears.* There were no paint supplies in this room, and it had a more studious look and feel to it than the previous room. The walls were lined with wooden bookshelves from floor to ceiling. Several old dusty books were lying here and there in clusters on the shelves. *Now this is my kind of room.* A few old cardboard boxes sat on the floor in front of the shelves. The flaps on the top of one of them were open and Seth could see that it was empty. The word "Books" on the side was lit by the moonlight coming in the window. It appeared someone had brought the box in here from the other room, along with a few others, and put all the books on the shelf. *How did they get in here? Did someone else do this?* Seth shuttered to think about the possibility of another person being in this house with him.

He took a few steps into the room and looked around. Near the window was an elegant high backed leather chair with rivets along the edges, along with a large wooden desk that was covered in books and papers. To the right of the desk sat a couple of old filing cabinets, whose drawers had slid halfway open. One drawer was sitting on the floor completely removed from the cabinet. Seth walked over to nose around a bit. The drawer was filled with hanging folders covered in dust and stuffed with documents of some sort.

Seth pulled the chair out from under the desk and brushed off the dust. *I wonder if it will still hold me.* After pushing down on it to test the sturdiness, he carefully sat down and leaned back. The leather creaked and stretched for the first time in a long time. It felt soft as it molded around him, and had held up well over the years.

From here he had a clear view out the window and wondered what it might have looked like on a bright sunny day under different circumstances. He closed his eyes for a second to imagine the darkness lifted off this place. He pictured the curtains swaying in the breeze coming in from the ocean. He pictured birds running through the sand and wading through the shallow blue water. When he opened his eyes, though, the images vanished and were replaced by the grim scene before him. The windows were broken in several places, and the air was cold and stagnant, filled with dust. The sand was as cold and motionless as the water, and everything he saw brought a feeling of hopelessness with it.

On the desk before him sat an old typewriter. It was large, black, and bulky. He had only seen typewriters such as this in photographs. In large white letters on the top read

"Underwood." The keys were circular and white, and several of the letters were worn down and barely readable. It had received plenty of use in its day. Papers covered the desk, along with several dusty old books.

He picked up a small tri-fold brochure that was covered in dust, held it to his mouth and gave a swift blow. Dust flew into the air and into Seth's face, bringing on an abrupt sneeze. His blow revealed the words and photos below the dust. He held the paper up and angled it towards the moonlight breaking through the window so he could read the words. It was some sort of brochure for a travel company. A large industrial looking cruise ship graced the front cover, along with several pictures of the ocean and the ship's accommodations. *The Marco Polo... cool name for a ship.* Seth scanned the photos and then read the tagline aloud, perhaps tired of the silence that hung around him. "Close Your Eyes and Picture the Most Sublime Place You Can Imagine..."

Seth smiled at the word sublime. It was always one of his favorites. He felt himself becoming calm, and stood up from the chair. He walked past the empty book boxes, out of the room, and back out of the beach house. He walked up to the edge of the water, where it met the sand. He stared out into the vast emptiness of the water, the brochure still clung tight in his hand. The darkness before him provided the perfect backdrop for imagination, a blank slate on which he could paint his vision. *The most sublime place I can imagine, huh?* Seth closed his eyes and spread his arms wide.

His thoughts took him to a tropical beach with palm trees growing everywhere. The sand stretched out before him to meet the waves with a crash. The water was a deep azure and the sky was crystal clear. He imagined the sun blasting its rays down onto his golden brown skin as the sweat beads gathered on his forehead. In his mind, he was standing there in the heat, feeling the warmth penetrate him, with his arms raised wide, palms up to the sun...

CHAPTER NINE

A BLACK BOX

     Seth stood in front of the dark waters with his arms spread wide. His eyes were closed, and the brochure was still firmly gripped in his hand. Visions of a sun-drenched sky were etched in his mind. He imagined his hair blowing in the warm breeze, making its way inland from far out on the ocean, bringing with it the scents of far off lands. He pictured the gulls and other birds wading in the crystal clear waters where the sand reached out to meet the sea and disappeared beneath its surface. He pictured a ribbon of green, made up of trees and vegetation that lined the coast for miles in each direction. A smile formed on his face as he basked in the glow of his fantasy, a stark contrast to the dark and desolate beach where he and the beach house now stood.

He held his eyes closed for several seconds, clinging to the images in his head for as long as he could, when it was interrupted by a sudden gust of air on his face. It was not imagined, and a far cry from the warm breeze in his sublime vision. It was bitter cold, and as it quickly passed over him, he felt the harsh bite on his skin. In an instant his whole body was engulfed in a wave of icy air, chilling him to the core, blowing his hair back. He opened his eyes and was struck by the surprising and unexpected view before him.

A monstrous iceberg, nearly twenty-feet high, was floating all alone in the brilliant blue water in front of him. It drifted slowly, about a hundred yards out. Seth, having never before seen an iceberg, couldn't take his eyes off of it. He stared at it with a childlike awe, and then turned to gather in the breadth of his new surroundings. He was most definitely not in front of the beach house anymore. Gone was the desk, the chair, and the brochure. Erased was the beach and the eerie beach house. In the blink of an eye, he had been thrust into a new world, and the entire view from where he now stood was surreal. It was like nothing Seth had ever seen before.

He was standing on one of the upper decks of a massive ship of some kind, cruising slowly through what appeared to be the Arctic or Antarctic Ocean. To Seth, it looked like an alien world or a different dimension, but at the same time, the beauty and serenity of it all calmed him and eased his fears. He simply looked around at the wonders in front of him. It was night, but the sky still had a soft blue glow to it, as if perpetually stuck at dusk. The bright moon cast a powerful light down on everything in sight. The most pristine blue waters stretched out endlessly to the horizon in every direction, and he could almost see the curvature of the Earth bending slightly in front of him. The sea was littered with numerous other icebergs floating in the water for as far as he could see.

They sparkled a brilliant white, and they varied in size from that of small automobiles to some the size of houses, and no shape seemed quite the same. Here and there, Seth spotted arches, mountains, and tunnels. It was an unbelievable and breathtaking sight.

The ship was massive, yet it made barely a sound as it glided through the water with ease. Seth walked to the edge and looked down over the railing. From where he stood, he was about sixty feet off the water and could see most of the ship. It was nearly the length of two football fields and was surrounded by water that seemed to stretch out forever in every direction. A strong gust of icy air blew hard on him, and the brochure slipped from his numbing hand and blew quickly out to sea. He watched it fly until it was out of sight, never seeming to land.

He placed his hands on the railing in front of him and was shocked by the extreme cold. The sights and wonders of this place had captivated him and kept his attention away from the climate. Only now did he realize how cold he actually was.

He took a moment to examine his attire. He didn't seem to be dressed for his current setting. On his feet, he wore fancy black polished dress shoes, above which were dark black pin striped slacks. On his upper body hung a white long-sleeve button-up shirt that also had tiny black pinstripes. It was made out of thin material and definitely not sufficient for the temperatures outside. The shirt was tucked into his slacks, and a belt completed the ensemble.

He looked around him for a winter coat to combat the cold but found nothing. He crossed his arms in front of him and hugged his sides as the cold air bit through his clothing. By now he was shivering intensely, and he reached his hands into the pockets of his pants to keep them warm. In the right pocket, he felt what appeared to be a plastic credit card and pulled it out to have a closer look. On one side there was a picture of a cruise ship under which the words "Marco Polo" were printed in fancy lettering. *Marco Polo? So it is real... I'm really here!* He flipped over the card to examine the other side. The background image on the back was a map of the world. Antarctica was outlined and had several stars pinpointing certain locations on the continent and in the surrounding waters. *Antarctica!? This is not what I imagined...* A magnetic strip was on one side and the numbers "215" on the other. He realized what it was. *Ahhhh, a room key!*

    Seth, encouraged by this new discovery, looked around for a way inside. He didn't know exactly where to go, but being on the top deck, he knew he needed to go down. He spotted a door with the word "Stairs" on the outside, weathered and worn from the harsh conditions they lived in, and hurried over to it. The movement brought much needed warmth to his muscles, but his hands and face felt as if they were practically frozen in place. He struggled to pull the door open against the strong winds, and his hands were numb to the touch of the metal door.

    Once inside, the door shut with a clang behind him. He looked over the edge of the stairs to the bottom far below. He hurried down to the next floor below him and looked at the door. *Level 5, three more to go.* As Seth descended step after step, turn after turn, he wondered what might be waiting for him inside room 215. His nerves began to tingle, and the adrenaline pumped through his veins. When he finally got to the door leading to Level 2, he paused for a second and took a deep breath. The air was slightly warmer in the stairway than on the top deck, but not by much.

    When he opened the door to Level 2, a rush of much needed warmth greeted him. On the other side he saw a long hallway that was lined with doors on either side. He looked at the door closest to him on the right. Small elegant brass numbers adorned the outside of the wood paneled door, just above the peephole. It read "236." The ship was so large that it was very steady and calm on the icy waters, navigating the icebergs easily without rocking or leaning. Had he not just experienced the upper deck above, Seth might have thought he was simply in a hotel somewhere.

He walked past room after room and vigilantly watched the numbers on the doors descend on each side, until he finally reached room 215 on his left. He stepped up to it and placed his ear on the door, listening carefully for any sound coming from inside. There was nothing. He pulled out the room key in his pocket and double-checked the number. *215.* The security lock on the door that held the card reader had a red light on it. He looked down the hall to his left and right, scanning for watchful eyes. He stood in front of the door deep in thought for several seconds as his curiosity and need for answers began to trump his fear.

Well, here goes. I hope no one is inside. Hesitantly, he slid the card into the slot and quickly pulled it out. He waited. After a nerve racking second and a half, Seth heard a clicking sound and the light on the security device turned green, granting him permission to enter. He slowly opened the door and took a peek inside. It was dark and quiet. He managed to say "Hello" through his cold numb lips, but no one answered. The sound of his voice was slightly deeper than he remembered, and his echo nearly sounded like someone else. He took a step inside the room and closed the door. As it shut, he heard the locking mechanism click again behind him.

The room was rather small and not unlike a hotel room, but more quaint and compact. A small lamp across the room gave a warm yellow glow to the space. There was a single bed straight in front of him and a bathroom off to the right. A stack of books lay on the floor next to the bed. On the bed were a few articles of clothing, including a very warm looking large winter coat. He walked over and picked it up. *This would have been nice a few minutes ago.* Under the coat was another room key, identical to the one he found in his pocket on the deck of the ship. *Someone else? Maybe they give you two. Who would I be here with?*

Next to the bed stood a chair and a small desk, which held the lamp that lit the room. Papers and pens littered the desk and on them sat a small laptop. He flipped through some of the papers and spotted a brochure for the cruise line. The logo matched the ship on the swipe card. Seth recognized it immediately and read the words under the logo under his breath. *"The Most Sublime Place You Can Imagine..."* The words reminded him of his vision of the tropical beach and the warm air blowing in his hair. *So much for being in the sun,* he thought.

Seth stepped through the doorway to the bathroom and clicked on the light switch on the wall next to the door. In a split second the light filled the room, and a man he did not recognize appeared instantly out of nowhere, standing directly in front of him. Their eyes met and Seth let out a shriek and ducked in fear. *Whoa!?!, what the...*

As soon as he ducked, the man in front of him also disappeared out of sight. Seth's heart pounded. He covered his head and stared directly into the floor. He panted heavily, but after a few seconds had passed, he realized his folly and slowly rose up. Embarrassment slowly set in. The strange man in front of him, though different and unrecognizable, was his own reflection in the mirror on the bathroom wall.

Seth stood in silence, staring at himself with his mouth slightly open. He closed his lips, and the man in the mirror followed suit. He reached his hand up and touched his face as he leaned in to take a closer look. He was different somehow... older. A few gray hairs stood out to him on his temples, and a few more were hidden among those on his chin. His face seemed fuller and more round. He stepped back to take a better look at his body in the mirror. He hadn't noticed on the deck of this ship, but he had put on a few pounds since college. He wasn't fat, but fuller and thicker, with more muscle. As he looked at himself in the mirror he felt more like an adult than he ever had before. More of a man. As a child he used to wonder what it was like to become a man. He was certain that a boy became a man when he turned eighteen. But when that day came and went for him, he felt no different. He still felt like a boy. So then he thought twenty-one was the age he would finally become a man. That year too came and went, yet he still saw a boy when he looked in the mirror. Perhaps it happens too slowly. Perhaps changes occur so subtly over time that it happens without recognition. Maybe a boy isn't supposed to simply wake up one day and feel like a man. Maybe those are just his dreams.

But for Seth, it did happen like that. This was that moment he had always wondered about. He looked in the mirror and suddenly felt like a man for the first time. He had a strange feeling that he was lost, but at the same time, an odd feeling like he was exactly where he was supposed to be. He stared at his new appearance, as questions began to fill his mind. *I wonder how old I am... or what year it is. And why am I on a cruise ship in the middle of Antarctica?*

As these thoughts consumed him, a sharp knock suddenly sounded on the cabin door. Seth shuttered a little and turned towards it, not certain what to do. *Who could that be? Is this not my room? Then how did I get the key?* He looked around for a place to hide but there was none. Seconds passed and the knock came again. There was nowhere to go. He would have to confront the situation. He took a hesitant step towards the door.

"Who is it?" he asked, hoping it was simply room service that he could make go away.

"It's me, open up. I don't have my key with me." The voice belonged to a woman. He turned and looked at the other room key that was lying on the bed. *I'm here with a woman...* Seth's hands trembled. The voice was soft and sweet, and somehow familiar, but he couldn't pinpoint the owner. He wasn't sure where he was or why he was here, but was fairly certain some of the answers he was seeking were on the other side of that door. He walked over to it and reached for the handle. When his hands touched the metal, he paused for a second and felt his heart racing in his chest. He peeked out the peephole, but couldn't see her face. She had her head turned, looking down the hall. He paused for a moment, then turned the handle and opened the door.

The door seemed to pass in front of Seth in slow motion, revealing the woman on the other side an inch at a time. She was a couple of inches shorter than him and slender, with an aura of elegance that surrounded her. She was wrapped in a large wool coat that was open in the front, giving hints of her silky black dress. Her hair was long and brown, with a slight wave to it, and he saw how it fell gently onto her shoulders. He knew the face immediately. His heart pounded and felt as if it was going to leap out of his chest. It was Sovannah.

Seth couldn't believe it. It was most definitely her, yet she was different. She was older now too, just as he was. They were both perhaps in their late twenties now, and she was even more beautiful than he remembered. He hadn't seen her since that amazing first kiss in college, and yet here they both stood, together on a cruise ship years later, in the middle of the Antarctic Ocean, as surreal and unbelievable as that sounded to him.

When she saw him her eyes lit up and her lips formed a smile. "I brought your hot chocolate!" She handed him a foam cup with a lid on it as she slipped by him into the room. He watched her walk by and marveled at how gracefully she moved. He shut the door and turned towards her. He stood there motionless, holding the cup, frozen stiff by the latest turn of events.

Sovannah looked at him in a way that told Seth they have known each other for a long time. To him, it felt like just yesterday that they were lying on the grass looking up at the stars together, but at the same time he felt that time had gone by. Lots of it. He could feel it. *What happened to the time in between? Have I been with her the whole time? Why can't I remember? Have I slipped into the future somehow?* The whole thing was like a dream to Seth, and he stood there with a look of confusion on his face.

Sovannah sat her cup on the desk next to the brochure and turned to him. "What happened to you, anyway?" Seth didn't really know how to answer. He just stood there with a lost look on his face. Luckily Sovannah's words kept coming, giving him a little time to think. "We were both standing on the deck looking at the icebergs and I went to get the hot chocolate. When I came back you were gone."

Seth's eyes wandered around the room and fixed on the coat lying on the bed. "I... came back down here to get my coat. I thought I would be back up there by the time you got back. I guess I got distracted." He felt the embarrassment again from the incident involving his own reflection and smiled. *Distracted...*

She smiled back and shook her head slightly. "I told you that you would need it, didn't I? I swear you never listen to me. You think you are so tough." She chuckled softly and turned to adjust her hair in the mirror. "The wind is really doing a number on my hair out there."

I never listen to her? I wonder how long we have been together... Clues to the questions Seth had inside were coming to him slowly. He still didn't know how he managed to jump into the future with Sovannah, or why they were on a ship on icy waters, but one answer was good enough for now. It seemed to ease his mind. Besides, he was with Sovannah again. She was the girl of his dreams, and being with her again felt like a dream coming true, and for now that was good enough.

Satisfied with her hair once again, Sovannah turned to him. "So, do you still want to get in the hot tub after dinner? Sounds fun to me... we can look at the penguins!" Her excitement seemed to fill the room.

Seth looked at her and spoke honestly, knowing to him the words meant something more. "Whatever you want to do sounds wonderful to me. I'm just glad to be with you. Right here. Right now. On this ship."

Sovannah stepped towards him with a loving look on her face. She put her arms around his neck pulled him closer. "You are such a sweetheart, you know that? I'm glad to be here with you too. This place is so amazing, and I wouldn't want to celebrate our anniversary any other way. Six years! Can you believe it? It seems like just yesterday that we met for the first time in college, you know?" She leaned in and gave him a little kiss on the lips.

"I definitely do," he said. *If she only knew...*

She grabbed her room key and walked to the door. "Now let's go, I think it would be fun to walk the entire length of the ship before our dinner reservation. We have about forty minutes, and I'm not sure how long it is going to take." Seth picked up the coat from the bed and threw it over his shoulder before following her out. His thoughts turned to the gray hairs on his temples again. *Six-year anniversary? Wow. Six years... That makes me twenty-eight...*

As Seth followed Sovannah down the hall to the stairwell, he thought about the beach and the beach house. He remembered the boxes and the dust, and the book. He remembered meeting Sovannah on that warm summer day in college, and waking once again in the sand afterwards. He was starting to wonder which place was real. *I was just there on the beach. I was just in college. How can I be twenty-eight now? Is this a dream?* The questions were beginning to overwhelm him.

"Are you okay, Seth?" It was the first time he heard her say his name out loud, and hearing it in her delicate voice seemed to ease his mind and wash away most of his anxiety. He might not know *where* or *when* he was, but at least he knew *who* he was. "You are being awfully quiet tonight. Are you sure you have your sea legs yet? The captain said it might take a few days."

A thought hit Seth that he hadn't realized until now. Although he had a lot of questions surrounding him, and was lost in his own mind, Sovannah was completely unaware of his situation. It was like she has been here the whole time somehow. *But where is here? Or when?* Seth knew he would have to start acting normal, at least on the outside. "I feel fine... I was just thinking about the last six years and how fast they seem to have gone by."

"I know! I can't believe it either. Six years already!" She opened the door to the stairwell and a rush of cold air hit them. Seth stopped to put on his coat before stepping over the threshold. Sovannah reach down and grabbed his hand as they walked up the stairs to the upper deck. "Your hands are always so much warmer than mine. I Love that." Her words immediately put a smile on Seth's face. Touching her hand again reminded him of the very first time their hands met, and of their first kiss. To Seth, it was the only kiss they have ever shared.

When they reached the door in the stairwell leading to the main ship deck, Seth pulled Sovannah back just before she opened the door. Without saying a word, he put his hands on her waist and gently spun her around. With his eyes full of passion, he pulled her close and kissed her deeply and strongly, as if he was trying to make up for six lost years in a single moment. He cupped the side of her face and pulled her close. It felt so small and delicate in his hands. Her fingers pressed into his back tighter and pulled him even closer.

After the kiss, she looked into his eyes and sighed. "There's the Seth I know."

He had a newfound pep after the kiss, and a smile that would be difficult to remove. He stepped past her and opened the door leading to the outside, letting in another rush of even colder air. They were on the highest full-length deck on the ship, where Seth first arrived here, and Sovannah squeezed his hand tighter just as the air hit her. "Let's go to the very front and look over the edge!" He watched her eyes light up as she said the words and he appreciated her excitement. He noticed changes in her since meeting her in college. With no memory of the last six years, Seth saw immediately the gradual changes that must have taken place over half a decade spent together. The young girl he met back then was all business and felt jealous of his childlike awe about nature and the stars. Six years later, she was the one who couldn't wait to see the penguins on the icebergs. He Loved it.

"We've been on this boat for four days and I'm still amazed!" Sovannah pulled him over to the railing on the side of the boat. "And I Love how it never really gets dark here. I don't think I could ever get bored with looking out on a blue sea and seeing icebergs floating by for as far as I can see. It's incredible."

Hand in hand, they walked towards the front of the boat, taking turns spotting interesting iceberg shapes and formations, and looking for animals in the water and on the ice. Here and there they saw penguins, seals, and various birds. They were like two high school kids experiencing Love for the first time. Seth was falling more and more in Love with her with each passing minute. *I could spend forever with her...*

They walked past the small ice-drenched lifeboats attached to the sides of the ship, stacked two at a time. The ropes had an inch thick icy skin on them, and looked like giant icicles. Two huge anchors were in their standby position out of the water and fastened to the deck of the ship. Their massive chains were coiled around large metal drums, waiting the next plunge into the frigid depths below. Each step they took had to be placed with care in their dress clothes.

When they arrived at the very front of the ship, Sovannah stayed back as Seth walked to the edge and peered over the rail to the water below. He watched as the massive hull cut through the water and pushed smaller pieces of ice away with ease. "You have to see this, Sovannah!" He reached his hand behind him but felt nothing, so he turned around and saw that she was standing about five feet back from the railing. "Are you scared?" Sovannah just nodded with a nervous look on her face. *How adorable,* he thought. Seth smiled and walked over to her. "I thought you were excited to look over the edge?"

Sovannah's face now showed a little embarrassment along with her nervousness. "I was, but... now that I'm here... it seems a little... scary."

Seth reached down and put his hand on hers. "Come on, I'll hold your hand the whole time." They walked very slowly over to the edge together and she found the courage to look down. She squeezed his hand tightly at first, but her fears soon subsided. They looked out to the horizon and let the cold air blow in their faces. "It almost feels like we are flying doesn't it?" Seth closed his eyes and spread his free arm out like a wing. Sovannah was not brave enough to close her eyes, and held on to his side. She saw the look of release and fearlessness on Seth's face and it made her smile.

After a few seconds, she looked down at her watch. "Okay, Leo, we should get back now. Our reservation is in ten minutes. Plus, I need to warm up my toes!"

Sovannah grabbed his hand and led the way towards the ship's dining area. They looked up at the giant captain's control room that rose high above the top deck. The lights shining down from above glistened in the thick sheet of ice that coated nearly everything on board. "It's beautiful isn't it? I bet the view is even better from up there." Seth nodded in agreement as they entered the ship and made their way towards the dining amenities on level four. *I'm glad she knows where we are going...*

"I've been looking forward to tonight, but it's so bittersweet." Sovannah had mixed emotions in her voice.

Seth wondered what she meant. "Bittersweet? How so?"

"Well, sweet because I'm really excited about our dinner at Maxim's. I've heard it's really amazing, and to be honest, I've been bored with the same food day after day in the Seven Seas Café. And I've been looking forward to tonight since we left port four days ago, when you promised a surprise. You said we would celebrate our anniversary in style and that I would never forget this one. How can a girl not look forward to that? But at the same time it's bitter... because I know that tonight is our last night on the ship."

Last night? Seth's heart sunk a little when he heard those words. To him it was the first night on the ship. But he tried his best to make her feel better. "I guess I didn't realize it... I suppose we will have to make the most of tonight then... and make a memory we will never forget."

Sovannah smiled as she opened the door to Maxim's. "Sounds wonderful."

As soon as they stepped inside, a large well-built Italian man in a red and white suit greeted them, as if he were waiting for them. He spoke with a deep Italian accent. "Good evening and welcome to Maxim's. May I please have your name, sir?"

"Seth."

"Ah yes, Seth. And this Lovely woman must be Sovannah. Come right this way, we have your private table all set up. I'm sure you will find it splendid. It is the finest table in the house." Sovannah's eyes got wide listening to the man and she looked at Seth, obviously impressed. Seth smiled back at her.

As they followed the Italian man to the table, they marveled at how gorgeous it was inside this place. It was somewhat dark, and very cozy. Nearly everything was red with elegant black trim. The isles were lined with accent lights, and the tables were lit by candlelight. High walls between each table gave them the resemblance of being in their own private little areas.

At the far end of the restaurant, nestled in the back, the man opened two fancy glass doors leading to a small room with a single table that was lit by several candles. A chandelier hung low over the table, which had a very nice arrangement of flowers on it. He stepped aside and motioned for them to enter. "Here you are. I hope you enjoy your visit with us today."

"Thank you." After the man left, Seth shut the glass doors, stepped over to one of the chairs, and pulled it out for Sovannah.

He could tell in her eyes what she was thinking but she said it anyways. "Such a gentleman." She slid off her coat and handed it to him, and sat down as he slid the chair in beneath her. He placed her coat on the back of one of the empty chairs around the table. She smelled the flowers on the table to verify their authenticity, then sat and looked around the room as he walked around to his side. She watched the shadows flicker on the wall from the candles, and smiled to herself. "This place is incredible. And the guy was right. This is the best table here. It's so romantic! How did you pull this off?"

It made Seth happy to see her so excited. "I'm not sure, but I'm glad you like it. Before we order, though, I need to find the restroom." Seth walked over to the glass doors. "Go ahead and pick out a bottle of wine if you'd like." He didn't really have to use the bathroom, but his heart and thoughts were racing, and he just needed a few moments alone to soak it all in.

As Seth walked to the bathroom he thought about the start to this day. He thought about opening his eyes for the first time on the ship and seeing the icebergs. He was scared at first, but amazed at how different he felt now. In a matter of an hour or so, all the confusion and fear he held inside had turned to complete content. He was with Sovannah again, and was reminded of his feelings for her. It was like Love at first sight happening all over again with the same girl. *But I've been with her for six years!*

Seth pushed open the bathroom door and walked to the mirror. The person looking back at him still felt like a stranger, but he was prepared for it this time. The questions in his mind continued. It was like he was living someone else's life momentarily. He fought off the panic that was building inside him. He stared deep into his own eyes in the mirror, trying to reconnect with himself on some level, trying to remember. He closed his eyes and took a few deep breaths, until his heart slowed and his nerves began to settle. He opened his eyes and the muscles in his face relaxed. *Who cares why or how you got here, let it go. You are with her and that is enough...*

When he opened his eyes, he noticed a small bulge in the jacket over his heart that he hadn't noticed before. He pat the area with his hand and felt something in the interior pocket of the coat. He unbuttoned the top three buttons and reached his hand inside. In the pocket was a small item shaped like a cube, which he pulled out to examine. It was a black box roughly two inches wide on each side. The top half of the box served as a lid that rested on a hinge at the back. He slowly opened the top, catching a glimpse of the sparkle beneath. Seth's jaw slowly dropped open. *A ring!?*

His nerves fired at will. His breath and heartbeat quickened their pace. The brief moment of calm he enjoyed a few seconds ago seemed distant. His hand was shaking as he pulled the ring from the case and closely examined it in the dim light of the bathroom. Even in low light it glistened like the ice on the deck of the ship.

Why would I have a ring? The moments leading up to this one offered clues to this latest question. *A cruise ship... Sovannah... our anniversary... an elegant dinner... our final night on the ship... a promised surprise...* It all made sense now. Seth put the ring back in the case, returned it to his pocket, and headed back to the table, his heart still racing.

Sovannah was pouring wine into his glass when he opened the glass doors. She smiled as he walked in. "They had our favorite red." She turned the label on the bottle towards her and read it aloud. Concannon Conservancy Merlot, 2008."

Seth put his coat on the back of his chair and smiled back at her. "Very nicely done."

"Isn't it amazing how we are in the middle of an icy ocean in Antarctica on a giant cruise ship, and yet sitting in this fancy restaurant we would have no idea what was outside these walls if we didn't already know. They do a good job of keeping everything so... compartmentalized."

"I know. It's crazy to think about. Every part of this ship seems like its own little secluded world."

The dinner seemed to pass by quickly as Seth was lost in his thoughts about the ring and its obvious implications. On the outside he smiled and chatted and ate his dinner, while inside his mind was elsewhere. The food and wine came and went as he acted out numerous possible scenarios inside. *I know what I came here to do now. I'm sure there was a plan, but what? When was I going to do it? How was I going to ask? Am I supposed to do it at dinner? Should I already have asked earlier? What words are the right words?* The questions and stories unfolded in his head as he imagined more and more ways to propose to her, desperately seeking the one that was intended for this night.

As the meal concluded, he remembered another detail about the evening, something Sovannah said earlier. Something about... *a hot tub. That's right, she wants to get in a hot tub after dinner and watch the penguins float by. Sounds like the perfect time. Maybe then...*

As they left the restaurant and said goodbye to the large Italian man at the door, Sovannah held Seth's arm in hers, and looked up at him with a Loving smile on her face.

"Thank you so much for dinner. For this whole trip actually. It's been the best week I can remember. And the best way I can think to finish it off is in one of the private hot tubs on the observation deck, with the icebergs floating by, and the stars above us! What do you think?"

Seth walked up to one of the elevators in the hallway and pushed the down arrow. "I think we should head back to the room and grab our suits."

He couldn't help but kiss her again when she stepped into the elevator and the doors shut. When they got to the room Seth swiped the card, this time with no hesitation, and led her inside. He took off his coat and threw it on the bed, somehow feeling as if he had done the same thing once before. "Should we put our suits on here or do they have a place to do that on the observation deck?"

Sovannah neatly hung her coat in the little closet just inside the door. She kicked off her shoes and walked into the bathroom, flicking on the light as she entered. "I'm not sure actually, I say we just change here and wear our long coats over the top. It's going to be cold until we get in though. Any idea what the temperature is outside?"

"I think I overheard somewhere that it was six or eight degrees below zero. Something like that. But the water should be a wonderful one hundred degrees. I can't wait!"

Seth took off his shirt and added it to the growing pile on the bed. "Any idea where my swim shorts might be?"

"I put most of your stuff in the bottom drawer the first day we got here. Check there."

Seth found the shorts and quickly changed into them, just as Sovannah's black dress flew out of the bathroom and landed on the bed. Anxious and nervous at the same time, he spun around to see her. The bathroom door was wide open and Sovannah was standing in front of the mirror removing her makeup. The only thing she was wearing was a lacy black bra and matching boy-short panties that clung to her hips, accentuating her curves. The light fell softly on her skin and glistened in her hair. The rest of the room seemed dark, as if the light chose only to land on her. Sovannah was the only thing that existed to Seth in this moment. Even he was lifeless, just another adoring object in the room. He stood in awe of her beauty.

    She turned and noticed him staring at her. "Six years and you still look at me like it's the first time you've ever seen me. That's why I Love you."

    Seth took a few steps closer to her as shots of adrenaline flowed through his body. "You look like an angel standing there in the light... the most beautiful thing these eyes have ever seen. And boy-shorts... I'm helpless around them."

    She smiled and called for him coyly. "Come here."

    Seth closed the gap between them. "And I Love you too."

    She pressed her warm body up against his. Her skin was soft and smooth, flawless to both the eyes and the hands. They kissed deeply and passionately, and then turned to look at themselves in the mirror, as couples tend to do. As Seth turned, he noticed a scar on his left side, near his back. He turned that side more towards the mirror to examine it.

    Sovannah ran her finger along the scar. "I still remember when you got that. The first time we went skiing together. Only a few months after we started dating. It was crazy. You had never even had skis on your feet before, but of course you took off like the daredevil you are. And after only a few seconds on the bunny slopes you decided to just jump right in and take off down the blue diamond trail, even though you barely even knew how to stop. I tried to tell you."

Seth enjoyed the stories about their past together. He had no memories of the events, but hearing about them for the first time in her voice was exhilarating.

"And when you inevitably crashed like I said you would, all I could do was laugh at you, until I realized you were really hurt. In fact, I thought you were faking it all the way until they loaded you into the ambulance."

Seth smiled and continued to rub his scar as she finished getting dressed. After she quickly slipped into her bikini, they grabbed their long coats from the closet. Seth covertly slipped the ring out of the dinner jacket and into the long coat, before taking her hand and heading to the observation deck. There were only a couple of hot tubs there, but most of the patrons of the ship were not adventurous enough to come up here in only swimwear, so they got little use in this part of the world. But for the brave souls who did, it provided a great experience and a story that would amaze most friends. Each tub was surrounded on two sides by a small wall meant to block some of the icy air, and massive amounts of steam hovered all around, creating a dreamlike feeling for the courageous who dared.

Sovannah smiled and shivered at the same time as they approached. "It's beautiful."

Next to the hot tubs Seth noticed a small heated bathhouse for changing and keeping clothing warm until it was needed again. "Hand me your coat and I'll put it in here." She handed him her coat and he laid them in the room, managing to slip the ring box into his hand before closing the door. With his free hand, he held hers as they slowly lowered themselves into the water. Discreetly, he sat the ring box outside the edge of the hot tub, safely hidden just out of view. The steam in the air provided ample cover.

"Oh my, it's glorious!" said Sovannah. Seth could only let out a sigh and take a deep breath. The water was enchanting, but it took a few seconds to get over the shock of their skin feeling over a hundred degrees difference in temperature between the air and the water. After fully submerging up to her neck, Sovannah slid over to Seth and leaned her back up against his chest. Her wet skin was slippery and soft, and Seth wrapped his arms around her and kissed her shoulder and neck. *How could I be so lucky?*

Seth could see his breath as he spoke. "We are in a hot tub... on a cruise ship... in the ocean... near Antarctica... with icebergs floating by... could this be any more unbelievable?"

"Only if there were penguins!" Sovannah let out a giggle, then closed her eyes and just savored the moment in his embrace. Seth held her tight, trying not to think about the ring sitting just a few feet away. He wanted to enjoy this time with her for a little while first. He still had questions about how he managed to jump so far ahead in life, with no memory of the last six years, but for now, the questions would have to wait. These moments were worthy of his full devotion and attention.

Minutes passed with ease, and the soothing and bubbling hot water relaxed every tired muscle in their bodies. They talked about the sky and the stars and the moon, recounting their first meeting in college again. Long durations of silence would wander away as they held each other. With each breath their eyelids became heavier and heavier. Seth lowered his head and rested it on Sovannah's as he held her tightly. They closed their eyes and felt the vibrations of the ship, and listened to the hum of the jets in the water. Their breaths and heartbeats seemed to synchronize and slow down. In unison they began to drift off...

CHAPTER TEN

NO THANKS NECESSARY

10:28 p.m.
Sept. 6th, 2002
Liberum Medical Center
Springfield, IL

Charlie was sitting in the surgery waiting room, still holding the boy's book of poetry in one hand, and his cell phone in the other. The chair was uncomfortable, and his body was starting to ache from the long day. He scratched his head and wondered what would arrive first, the doctor with the results of the boy's operation, or the family who was currently on the way to the hospital from wherever they were when that moment came. The moment they heard the terrible news about their son.

As he waited, he thought about his son Michael. He could remember exactly where he was when his own terrible moment came. He remembered the call about his son's accident, the song that was on the radio in the truck, even the shapes of the individual stains on the shirt he was wearing that day. It was all frozen in time for him. And he knew the family would also hold onto the details in their own moment if the boy didn't make it. He knew what would happen if they never got to say goodbye. It would become etched in their memory. A scene they couldn't erase.

Ever since his son's accident, Charlie mostly felt numb and tired, but the anticipation of sitting in the room at this moment waiting on the news brought levels of anxiety to him that he hadn't felt in months. It awakened nerves and tensions that he had been holding down under blankets of guilt. He wished for the boy's life, but also, and maybe more so, for the swift arrival of the boy's father. He was all too familiar with the regret and solitude that comes from not being there for your son, and it wasn't something he would wish upon anyone. Even if deep down he knew there was nothing he could have done for Michael that night, as a parent he still pictured him lying there alone and scared, waiting for his end, and it ate away at him like a poison. Maybe that's why he was here right now. As a father, he felt an instinctual need to protect, or at the very least, to comfort a child who was going through a scary moment. But more than anything, one thought has repeated in his mind over and over the last seven months... *I wish I could have said goodbye.* He only hoped that in the event of bad news accompanying the doctor tonight, the boy's father might be here to get his chance at goodbye, the way he never did.

#

Down in the main entrance to the emergency room, the automatic doors opened with a rush as a frantic family rushed through them shoulder to shoulder, racing up to the counter with shared panic on their faces. The first to arrive was the boy's mother, a blond woman about 5'4", in her early fifties. Her quick movements were awkward, owing to the bad knees and osteoarthritis that she inherited from her own mother, and eventually passed on to her own children. Under her watery eyes were heavy bags that puffed out and held the teardrops for a moment before they fell down her cheeks. The bags weren't solely the result of this night, but earned through three decades of parenthood, worrying, and tragedy, that life and raising three children brought.

Rushing in immediately beside her, as if competing in a race for answers, was her daughter and the boy's sister, Michelle. She carried herself with a confidence and leadership that seemed to show itself more prominently during crisis times. As the oldest of the three children in the family, and a mother and wife herself, she was strong-willed and had a tendency to fall into the leadership role when the rest of the family was bothered or hesitant. She seemed to all who met her much older than her count of years, and captured the respect of people older than herself. She held her mother's hand as they approached the reception desk.

Just behind the two women of the family came Michelle's husband Brian and their two children, Marcus and Mariah. Marcus was quiet for a thirteen-year-old boy, and his face showed very little emotion aside from a wry smile that hinted at troublemaking at all times. Mariah on the other hand had to continually wipe the tears off her cheeks. The family was close, and she was especially fond of her oldest uncle, even though they lived a few hours apart. As a nine-year-old little girl, she was incapable of hiding her emotions, and her fear and innocence easily showed in her eyes. Brian held her hand to calm her, but her eyes stayed wide and fearful. Brian was a tall man with a young face, who seemed to be in a good mood no matter what the circumstances held. He had one of those mouths that even at rest seemed to hold a slight smile, and thus maybe contributed to his overwhelming popularity and likeability wherever he went.

Michelle turned to Brian. "Where are Ryan and Rachel? Isn't Dad with them? Why aren't they here?" Just as the words left her mouth, as if on cue, Ryan and Rachel rushed through the ER doors. Ryan was the boy's younger yet taller brother, and most people who saw them together incorrectly assumed he was the older of the two boys. Ryan recently got married to a small little blond girl named Rachel, who mostly kept quiet and presently clung tightly to his arm as they rushed up to the counter.

Behind them a bit, and moving slower than the rest, was the boy's father, Arthur. He was a retired baby boomer in his late fifties, and from the way he walked you could tell he had worked very hard throughout his life to support the family. The fact that he worked outside with his hands since he was a young man himself was an obvious deduction for those who looked closely at his skin, fingers, and brow. The years had made his joints a little tighter, and his movements a little slower, offering him many chances to complain, though he never did. He was proud and strong, like most fathers of his generation, and wanted the world to know it. He worked hard in his life to support this family, and he was unwilling to show weakness. Yet as the years toiled on, it became harder and harder for him to conceal it. Arthur's hair was fully gray, but had been since he was in his late twenties. No one who knew him could ever really tell his age. He was one of those people, like Bob Barker or older black men, who never seemed to age.

He was perpetually the same, both physically and emotionally, like a rock for his family.

As Arthur neared the front desk with the rest of the group, the boy's mom grabbed the attention of the nurse and tried her best to get some words out. Tears and gasps often interrupted her shaky voice. "My... son... is here. There was... an accident." As she sniffled, the words got trapped in her throat, and it became harder and harder for her to speak or see through the tears. The nurse seemed to be getting impatient.

Michelle ushered her mother over to Arthur. "Dad, take care of mom."

Arthur put his arm around his wife and turned her aside, allowing her to burst out in tears and crying under his protection. Although uncertain and worried himself, he played the support role without showing it. "It'll be ok, I promise. Let Michelle handle everything. We'll see him soon, I'm sure he's going to be fine. He's a fighter."

Michelle's words could be heard behind him. "We are here to see my brother..." She pointed to her mother, who was still crying into Arthur's shirt. "...and those are his parents. He was in a car accident near his college. He was brought here in an ambulance about an hour ago."

The nurse listened and spoke in a very robotic, business like tone that offered no sympathy. "What was his age and last name?"

"Twenty-two. Ashling."

The nurse hammered away at her keyboard and stared at the screen. Eventually it came to a stop. "I have an Ashling in the system. Twenty-two years old."

Upon overhearing her son's name, the boy's mother burst out crying even louder than before. Until now she had clung to the slim hope that it was all a mix-up, and her son was just out for a drive. Maybe someone borrowed his car. Maybe someone stole it. Maybe the boy in the accident was someone else. But now it was real. Michelle answered. "That's him. Is he okay?"

The family silenced in unison and hung on the receptionist's words. "He's currently in surgery. I'll call down and have a nurse come get you. She will lead you down to the surgical waiting area. Until then please have a seat over there and she will be here in a few minutes."

Each one found a seat and slumped into it in silence, occasionally sharing a glance that showed their concern, when they no longer could find the right words.

#

Back in the surgical waiting area, Charlie was still the only person in the room. He was sitting with his eyes shut when nurse Pineida opened the door.

"Hey, Charlie, the boy's family is here. I'm heading down to get them and bring them back here. Thought I'd give you the head's up."

Charlie thanked her as the door quickly shut behind her. He placed the boy's poetry journal back in the box, and slipped his cell phone back in his pocket. He rubbed his eyes and walked over to the soda machine, hoping a little caffeine would help him out. *Two dollars? Wow. No compassion, I swear. Feeding off the desperate.* As he inserted the bills, his grogginess began to quickly fade and his nerves began to tingle in his spine. Part of him was relieved that the family had made it, and that he wouldn't have to face the doctor by himself, in the event that the news was bad. But he knew that many questions would soon come his way. They would all want answers. *What am I going to say to them?* He walked to the window and stared out into the night for several minutes, trying to find the words. The rain had nearly stopped. The room seemed quieter now than ever. He could hear his own heart beating deep inside his ear, and he listened to the quiet cadence of his own lifeline, beating in rhythm with the second hand on the clock above him.

The silence was broken when he heard the door behind him open. He turned to look as the family poured into the room in a hurried and jumbled group. As they entered, he watched their faces. Each one carried a different variation of the same things: sadness, anxiety, hope...

Nurse Pineida stepped into the middle of them all. She motioned over to him. "Charlie, I'd like you to meet the young man's family." Charlie turned and tried to stand tall and proud as he walked toward them, as he once had as a young fireman. He flashed a sympathetic half-smile across his face. "Charlie's a firefighter here in Springfield. He was on the scene of the accident. He was the man who pulled your boy from the car tonight." The mother's lip was shaking as she heard the words, and her sniffling grew louder. "He didn't want him to be alone so he volunteered to wait with him here at the hospital and hang on to his belongings until you all got here."

Charlie reached out his hand to shake the father's. "Nice to meet you."

With tears still streaming down, the mother looked up at Charlie. "I'm Gail and this is Arthur. Thanks so much for saving my boy."

"No thanks necessary, ma'am. I'm not a savior, just did my job the best I could. If it wasn't me, it would have been one of the other guys."

"Well, thank you, anyway."

Charlie smiled and nodded as they all sat down, except for Marcus and Mariah, who went across the room to look out the windows and avoid the emotional adult talk. The rest gathered around Charlie, hoping to hear more details. Nurse Pineida opened the door, and spoke just as Charlie opened his mouth. "Surgery is nearly halfway done, but the doctor said he will be down to go over the details with everyone now that you've arrived."

As she left the room the focus shifted back to Charlie, who could sense the family's need for information, no matter how helpful it might be. He wasn't sure what to say, but knew he had to offer something. "He was awake when I found him."

Michelle became the voice for the family once again. "What happened? We heard such a quick version of the story. The cops said he drove his car into a river or something. How did it happen?"

"I'm not sure really. But the car never made it to the water. When we showed up it was stuck in a tree over the edge. We lowered the ladder down to the car and I climbed down to pull him out. He was actually awake when I got to him, but as soon as we made it to the top he collapsed, and was out cold the whole trip over here in the ambulance."

Michelle tried to offer any positive spin she could to her mother. "See, Mom, he was awake. That's good news." She turned back to Charlie. "Could you see how bad was he hurt?"

"He hit his head pretty good, but I'm not sure what else. It's all sort of a blur really. On the ride over here I think I heard something about a broken rib and maybe a punctured lung too, but the doctors seemed mostly concerned with his head." Charlie hesitated before the next sentence, knowing it would be hard to hear, and wishing he wasn't the one who had to deliver all of this information. "I think Miss Pineida said he's got a crack in his skull and that's why they rushed him to surgery. I think they are trying to reduce the swelling and pressure from the blood. I'm sorry... I wish I knew more, or had better news for you all. But the nurse said they have the best doctors in the country here. So at least he's in good hands. And now his family is here with him too. That's really important." For a moment, Charlie seemed to drift off again, thinking about the past.

The details brought a wave of even more fear and panic to Gail. It seemed all she heard were the negative words. Broken, punctured, swelling, pressure, BLOOD. She cried aloud at each one, before burying her face in Arthur's shirt again. A tear also left Michelle's eye and started a slow path down her cheek. "Mom, I'm sure he'll be okay. He's always been okay, no matter what has happened to him. He's tough. I'm sure he'll make it through this too just fine."

Arthur squeezed Gail and basically repeated everything Michelle had just said. "We'll see him soon." he added.

Everyone sat down after Charlie had finished, and tried to pass the time as best as they could, as they waited to hear from the doctor. It had only been roughly thirty minutes since nurse Pineida left them, but under the circumstances, each minute felt like ten, and the room seemed to shrink with every tick of the clock. Michelle and Gail were starting to get agitated.

Finally the silence was broken when the door opened and a tall doctor walked. He was dressed entirely in white with a stethoscope around his neck and a folder in his hand. Brian thought to himself that this look was mostly for the patient and the doctor's own ego, more for show than actual use. *Do they really use those stethoscopes all day?*

"I'm guessing you are all here for young Mr. Ashling?" he said, without really making eye contact with anyone, his eyes focused on the folder in his hands.

"Yes." Michelle stared straight at the doctor in anticipation. Gail's eyes were fixated on the floor below her, unable to make eye contact. Arthur squeezed her hand.

The doctor sat in the chair directly across from Michelle and looked each of them in the eye as he spoke, alternating between them and the contents of the folder. "Hello. I am Doctor Kaplan. I have been taking care of your son. He is still in surgery, which will most likely last another hour at least. While that is in progress, I'd like to go over the extent of his injuries with you, and tell you what steps we have taken up to this point, okay?" Michelle and Arthur nodded. "During his accident, he sustained several cuts and abrasions on this upper body. He also has a broken rib and a punctured lung, probably from the jolt of the initial fall in the vehicle. This could be from hitting the steering wheel or the dash. However, none of these injuries are life threatening, and they were initially treated in the ambulance on the way to the hospital. They will require more attention after surgery, but for now we will concentrate on more important things. Our major concerns are the injuries to the head. He suffered a major concussion, and an x-ray showed a small depression fracture in his cranium above his left eye near the hairline."

Gail let out another cry when she heard these words. Even Mariah, who didn't understand most of what she heard, was hanging on every word as she clung to her mother.

"A CT scan of this area showed damage to the soft tissue of the frontal lobe of his brain. This, in turn, caused bleeding and pressure inside his head. It was this pressure that caused him to black out at the scene of the accident. When this was determined, we immediately scheduled an emergency brain surgery to relieve the pressure and remove any bone fragments left behind, which may cause even more damage to his brain."

Michelle spoke up first, with tears in her eyes. "Is he going to be okay?"

"We are confident the surgery will be a success, but

there are no guarantees. To be honest, there's no way to really tell how much damage his brain sustained, or what lasting effects might linger afterwards. I'm sorry, but that's all the information I have at the present time. I'll know more when surgery has completed, and once he's in the recovery room I'll come back here and take you all to see him. Unfortunately, there's nothing you can do except wait at this point. It shouldn't be more than another hour or so. If you need anything, the nurse's station is just down the hall." He shook her hand and stood up. "I'll see you again soon."

    The group thanked him in unison before he left the room. As the door shut, Michelle put her arm around her mother. "Did you hear what he said? They are confident about the surgery. He'll be all fixed up in an hour and we'll get to see him, okay?" Gail sniffled and gave a silent "yes" with her nod, trying her best to focus on the good news.

CHAPTER ELEVEN

BITS AND PIECES

As Seth faded back from the warm bubbly water of the hot tub, he still clung to thoughts of holding Sovannah close in that steam filled oasis on the Antarctic cruise ship. As if coming back from a dream, his mind hung on while his body began to discover the change in his surroundings. His skin slowly dried and the warmth of the water evaporated with the escaping moisture. He opened his heavy eyes slowly and peeked out, fearing what he might see, and hoping for Sovannah.

A sinking feeling quickly filled him as the scent of her hair vanished in the air. The hot water was replaced by cold dry sand and Sovannah was nowhere in sight. He sat with his back to the dark waters, staring with disbelief at the beach house that stood before him again.

Not again! Was it all a dream? Am I dreaming now? He slapped his face as hard as he could. One side and then the other. Smack! "Wake up!" Smack! "Wake up!" He shouted into the darkness. "Sovannah!" Nothing returned to him. "Sovaaannnah!" Silence.

When it sank in that he was back on this dark, lifeless beach, his head lowered and he stared below him at the sand. He felt the weight of this place pushing down on him, both emotionally and physically. He felt weaker and more hopeless than the last time he was here. He had even more questions and even fewer answers. Time became meaningless to him. There was no timeline to follow, no explanation of the gaps, and no way of knowing if he would ever leave this place again, or if he really ever left before.

Think, dammit, think! He urged himself on, trying to make sense of it all. His thoughts ran in circles, but constantly came back to one image. *Sovannah.* Seth thought about the day he met her in college and how they marveled at the stars that night. Somehow his memories of that night felt dated to him, as if they were memories from long ago. He thought about the cruise ship and seeing her for the first time again in the cabin. He thought about their candlelit dinner and then their enchanting moment in the hot tub on deck. He could still smell the faint scent of her wet hair and the slippery touch of her skin under the water. He wanted so badly to be back in that moment with her.

Anger started to push out his other emotions one by one. Anger at being pulled back here to this place again. Anger at losing Sovannah again. Anger at his total lack of control. Anger at not knowing who or what was responsible for everything that was happening to him. He rose to his feet, and tears moistened his fiery eyes, as the anger could no longer be contained. His knees seemed weaker and harder to stand on.

"Why!" He shouted at the top of his lungs. "Why are you doing this to me?" he shouted over and over again until he fell to his knees and buried his head in his hands. *What is happening to me?* The tears poured down and disappeared into the sand. He sat for several minutes, replaying the events of the last time he was with Sovannah, hoping he would find a clue. He remembered nothing between his first kiss with her in the grass and his time with her on the ship. He remembered nothing between the cold of Antarctica and the isolation of this beach. Yet the memories of her in those two places were vivid. Her skin as he touched her hand for the first time... her lips as they trembled when he first kissed them... her eyes when she saw the candles at dinner... her hair as it soaked up the mist... all of it. *But was it all real? How could I have imagined all that?*

    Seth stood and turned his eyes to the beach house, with his hands on his sides. The fire in his eyes seemed to have cooled from the tears, and now housed an inquisitive look. He stared at the house as if he was staring into the eyes of his enemy, looking for weakness, looking for an advantage. His fingertip felt an aberration on the skin of his lower back, and quickly pulled away. He felt it again and knew what it was. His eyes grew wider and he clenched his teeth.

    He leapt forward and ran at full speed up to the steps outside the beach house. He took long strides and took the steps two or three at a time, rushing up to the door. *I need a mirror!* He ripped open the main door that was barely hanging on and it crashed to the wood behind him. He stepped into the kitchen and rushed to the other side, heading for the entryway to the dining room. He had been in here only twice, but felt like he knew this place well. When he reached the dining room he slid to a stop. The look on his face changed to confusion. He turned around and took another look in the kitchen.

Something is different, he thought to himself as he looked around the room, examining the contents, trying to remember exactly what it was like the last time he was here. "The cabinets!" He spoke the words aloud as he realized that last time he was here all the cabinet doors were crumbled and in ruins on the floor, but now the cabinets looked as if they had all been repaired. In fact, they looked newer. He opened one of them, and noticed there were dishes stacked neatly together on the shelves. Plates, glasses, bowls, etc... *What? Who did this?* He stepped back and shut the cabinet door, turning to continue his quest for a mirror. He hurried through the dining room into the main living room, which was empty. Again he looked around noticing the differences. *The boxes... they are all gone. Someone has been here... Someone has been unpacking!*

When he reached the bathroom he still had tears in his eyes. The mirror was covered in dust and the room was dark. He knew what he felt on his back, but still needed to see it to believe it for some reason. His eyes were the last things he could trust, and he was quickly losing faith in their honesty, too. He walked over to the window and grabbed the curtains with both hands. Instead of opening them he simply ripped them off the wall in one massive tug, letting them crash to the ground along with their metal support. His confusion had been slowly turning to anger since the first time he woke up on this beach.

With the moonlight flooding the room, he walked back over to the mirror and stood in front of it. He was motionless and could only see bits and pieces of himself through the dust on the glass. He stared at this blurry mosaic of himself, and realized that what he saw finally matched what he felt. His life had also become a blurry mosaic of itself, and he too had become only fragments of himself. He seemed to be living in bits and pieces, with no control, and no way to put it all back together. He worried he might never snap out of it. A tear built up in each eye and then began to trickle down his face.

He reached out his hand and wiped away a single swipe of dust through which he could now see his face. Just like on the cruise ship with Sovannah, he was older than the last time he was here. He pulled his shirt over his head and used it to wipe most of the dust from the mirror. He then turned and looked at this lower back over his shoulder. He felt the scar with his fingers as he examined it in the mirror, running his fingers along the contours. It was most definitely not imagined. *So it did happen. I did see her again. I'm 28 now... But I was just here yesterday.*

His head dropped and he closed his eyes. The tears dripped off his face and landed in the sink. It was so quiet that he heard the drops hit the dust covered ceramic one at a time. *I was just here* he thought to himself. *How did I get here? Why can't I remember?* Then he spoke the words out loud. "I was just here." He said it again louder, his voice filling the room. "I was just here!" He raised his voice and anger started to boil in his veins once again. "Why am I here?!" He lifted his head and stared into his own fiery eyes. "What is going on?!" He screamed at the unfamiliar face in the mirror, hoping for an answer. "Answer me!" He balled up his fist and slammed it down on the sink and the sound echoed through the house. Dust flew up into the air and the moonlight seemed to freeze the particles in the air.

"I'm not crazy," he said to himself aloud in a low voice, as if trying to convince himself of its truth. "I just want to wake up... I need to wake up." He stared into his own eyes as if trying to recognize himself, the way a person might look at someone they know they've seen before, but cannot remember where.

"Wake up," he said to the man in the mirror, who spoke back to him in unison. "Wake up!" He shouted the words as loud as he could and tears of anger and fear filled his eyes. "Wake up!! Do it! Just wake up!!!" His anger swelled. Again he balled up his fist and this time slammed it into the mirror as hard as he could. The man in the mirror mimicked his actions, and their two fists met in one fierce motion. The silvery glass seemed to explode on contact. The sound was deafening as broken pieces flew into the air in slow motion, lit by the soft white light of the moon, before falling all around him in a loud crash. He crumpled to the floor and wept.

The blood flowed out of his fist, but he felt no pain. He simply stared at it, watching the pale grayish-red fluid roll down his skin through wet eyes. His lashes were so filled with dust that the tears clumped around his eyes and hovered in front of this vision. His face pressed into the rug beneath him and he watched the blood make its way to the edge of his hand and slowly drip onto the fibers below. As he lay there in a crumpled ball on the floor, the barely visible colors in the room seemed to fade all around him into a dull mix of various shades of gray. He stared at the pattern on the rug and traced the lines with his eyes only inches away. The lines swirled together and moved around like a maze. He followed the openings from one section to another, trying to find his way out. It was one dead end after another. He closed his eyes and forgot about his hand. He rubbed his bloody fingers back and forth on the rug feeling the texture of the fabric as he tried to clear his mind. Maybe if he could just focus on his sense of touch with all he had, everything else would go away, if just for a moment. He didn't want to think anymore. No more puzzles, no more mazes, no more questions.

He exhaled deeply. His heartbeat slowed. Everything was quiet. Everything disappeared. Only the rug existed.

Then one thought came to him... One emotion grabbed hold of him... One thing appeared in his mind among the emptiness gave him peace... Sovannah.

CHAPTER TWELVE

FORTUNE COOKIES

Images of Sovannah fluttered around inside Seth's head seemingly at random. He was swimming in a sea of thoughts, of memories, and of dreams, and by now he couldn't discern one from another. Memories became dreams, dreams became memories, and thoughts bounced back and forth from one to the other, and often he wondered which was which.

He felt the rug again with his fingers. What was once cold, dusty, and moist from the blood of his fingers now felt soft and warm. The fibers were dry to the touch and his hand felt fine. He rubbed his finger where it was cut and felt nothing. He knew what it meant before he opened his eyes. *I've left again...*

When he did open his eyes, the rug was hanging in front of him, bright and new. The colors were vibrant, and the maze pattern was easily readable. For a few seconds he lost himself in the maze again before finding the way to the edge. He pulled his hand back and looked up. The rug was one of many that were hanging neatly from a mounted rack on the ceiling. Additional racks were to his left and his right. He saw a small tag attached to the rug near the corner.

"The Furniture Gallery"

Seth flashed a puzzled look on his face. *Doesn't ring a bell.* Wondering where he might be, he reached for the tag to inspect it for an address. A shine on his finger snatched his attention away from the rug. *A ring!* He pulled his hand back and brought it closer to his face. The ring was silver or brushed metal of some kind, and dimpled slightly, like the surface of a golf ball. It glistened somewhat in the light. He removed it from his finger to examine it more closely, and noticed some words etched on the inside of the loop.

"If not for You, for nothing shall I live. If not for You, my heart has naught to give."

He smiled when he read the words, and placed the ring back on his finger. *Left hand... third finger...* The clues were easy enough to put together. *I'm married. To whom? Maybe I proposed on the ship after all...*

A smile formed on his face without his knowing, as the pictures of the hot tub flooded his eyes. *Sovannah! Maybe she's here...* He ran to the edge of the isle and looked all the way towards the other side of the furniture store. She wasn't in sight. He quickly began walking down the main isle checking every offshoot and subsequent path in the store. His head bounced back and forth and his steps were quick and light, yet his ankles seemed weaker. Adrenaline pumped through his veins and his heart jumped up to a higher gear. Halfway through the store he still hadn't seen her, and he had nearly knocked over three people on his way. Sovannah had become his sole purpose, and finding her his only goal. In a whirlwind of jumbled experiences, she was the common thread.

As he reached the last isle he came to a stop. He hadn't found her and he had looked down every isle. Possible explanations all vied for thought in his head. *Maybe I dropped her off somewhere. Maybe she's waiting in the car. Maybe she's at home and I came here alone. Where is home? Maybe it's not even Sovannah. Maybe I married someone else? What am I doing in a furniture store? Am I supposed to be getting something? Should I leave? But where would I go? I don't even know where I am. Or WHEN I am.*

He noticed windows to his far left and headed towards them. The sun was low in the sky and would be setting within an hour or so. The light came in at a shallow angle, casting his shadow nearly twenty feet behind him, and making it hard to see without squinting. He covered the sun with his hand and looked out of the building in all directions. Nothing looked familiar to him.

"Looking for something in particular?" A woman's voice came from behind him. Seth turned around slowly, as his heart raced. He didn't know what he expected to find when he turned around, but he was anxious. The woman he saw had a big smile on her face. She was dressed in a black business skirt, and her hair was long and hung in front of her.

"Wh...what do you mean?" Seth was confused by the strange way the woman was looking at him and smiling so big.

"Are you looking for a new sofa? A bedroom set? Or perhaps a new rug? We have several items on sale today. I'd be happy to help you find what you are looking for." As she tilted her head, her hair revealed her name badge on her lapel, catching Seth's eye. *Kelsey.*

"No thanks Kelsey, I was just leaving." Seth stepped past her and aimed for the door at the front of the store. A few steps past her he stopped, and turned back towards her. "Could you answer one strange question?"

"Sure!" She seemed oddly excited about it.

"What city are we in right now?" Seth spoke slowly, and anticipated a look of condescension or disapproval from her, based on the obviously odd question.

"We are in Bloomington!" She smiled and seemed happy with herself as if it was a game show and she had just made it to the next level. Seth nodded his head and raised his lower lip up over his top one, confused by her tone.

"Thanks." He began to turn back towards the door and then stopped. Again he turned back to her. "Illinois or Indiana?"

"Indiana." She flashed a big smile again, giving Seth the impression that somehow he had just made her day a little better. *Strange woman...*

He turned again and headed for the front doors, this time not pausing until he reached them, flung them open wide, and stepped out into the sun. As the warmth of the rays hit his face, he closed his eyes and raised his arms in a V. There was something about being outside with sunlight on his face that always had the power to freeze him, to hold him in an eternal embrace, and to lift him away from the world and his troubles. He stood there in silence for several seconds. The insides of his eyelids filled his sight with a red glow.

He opened his eyes and turned to face the building. A slight breeze was in the air, and it was crisp with a touch of cold. A few leaves moved along the pavement in front of him, pushed by the breeze, and brown from the changing of the seasons. He looked around at the trees and their deep reds and oranges. It was that magical time of year when the summer was reluctant to pass the torch to the fall, and for two weeks the world offered perfection with its beauty, temperature, calmness, and peace that you couldn't dislike if you tried. Seth said to himself what nearly everyone says during these times. *Every day should be like this...*

    The Furniture Gallery was lit up brightly on the facade of the building in red letters. He looked around and felt familiarity, but couldn't pinpoint exactly where he was. The air was filled with sounds of cars and traffic, of birds and bugs. The buildings were spread to the right and left in standard strip-mall design. To the left was a small bakery and deli. The scent of fresh baked bread was in the air and caught Seth's attention. He couldn't remember the last time he felt hunger, but the wonderful smell swirled around him until his body began to crave it. To the right of the furniture store was a mega bookstore, which contained another smell that Seth couldn't resist - the smell of a brand new book opened for the first time. He walked closer to the windows and peered inside. He could see all the shelves and isles filled with books. The site made him pause and wonder what might be inside the covers of all those books. What amazing stories that will inevitably go unknown to him. The shelves were filled with thoughts and experiences he might never have. Filled with the ideas of other people. Filled with different emotions, different places, different times, and different worlds. It was overwhelming to him, and he stood there for a minute, lost in his own thoughts.

    "I knew I couldn't keep you away from the book store." Her words jolted him from behind, and his eyes immediately doubled in size. Without seeing her, he knew it was Sovannah. Her voice seemed to eliminate all other sounds, and shrink the world to whatever distance was between them. "What are you doing out here anyway?"

Seth turned around quickly, anxious to see her again. The perfection of the day seemed to wane in comparison to her beauty. She was wearing a light, but long-sleeved beige fall jacket that had two rows of large black buttons running down the front on either side, guiding one's eyes down the curves of her body. The curves were more visible due to the deep orange belt that was loosely tied around her waist and held the coat snuggly to her sides. On the front of the belt was a large bow, and to her side hung a small bag that was bright yellow and covered in intricate buckles and flaps. Below her waist she wore pants that may have been denim, but were tightly clung to her legs sticking out from under her coat, and colored a sort of dark olive green or brown that seemed to disguise their true material. Her legs disappeared into tall leather boots that matched her belt and rose up her leg more than halfway to her knees.

Her hair was long and brown, but lighter than Seth remembered, due to a long summer of being drenched in the sun by the pool. Her skin was darker, for the same reason. Some of her hair was inside her jacket, some on her shoulders, some held back by her sunglasses on top of her head, and several pieces were blowing gently in the breeze. Her hands were on her hips and her elbows were jutting out, and she spoke in an obviously sarcastic, bossy tone. "I go to the bathroom for two minutes and you try to sneak away and leave me." Her smile and her pouty lips gave away her playful and flirty tone, and Seth Loved every second of it.

"Sorry, I just wanted to soak up some of this sun before it goes down." He smiled back at her. "It's amazing outside."

"I know. I'm sorry we have to do this on Sunday. We probably shouldn't have waited until the last day, but it's been a crazy week. I'm so excited though! Aren't you?"

Seth didn't have a clue what she was talking about, but figured it was easier to simply agree now and figure the rest out later. "Of course I am."

"Our first night in our new apartment! Let's rent a movie and order Chinese!"

"That sounds like heaven." Seth could see the excitement in her eyes, and Loved how they lit up with every smile. "By the way, you look amazing. In fact, I don't think you've ever looked more beautiful than you do right now, right here, in this moment."

She took her hands off her hips and reached out to grab his. She squeezed and rubbed her thumbs on the tops of his hands. "How do you do it?"

Seth smiled back at her. "How do I do what?"

"You always know exactly what to say. You can take something as small as standing in the sun in front of a furniture store and make it... romantic. I Love that about you." She reached up and put her hands on the side of his face and pulled his lips to hers. As they pressed together Seth held her waist and pulled her even closer. The kiss was quick but passionate, only two seconds long and an eternity to him at the same time. After they parted, Seth's eyes remained closed for a few more seconds, trying to hold on to the moment as long as he could, like a boy reluctant to wake, trying to hold on to a good dream for a few seconds longer. "Now let's go back inside and you can show me the rug you picked out."

They spent the next hour walking the isles of the store, holding hands like two teenagers in the mall. They often stopped abruptly when she saw something else that caught her eye and inevitably got her even more excited than she already was. Seth joked with Sovannah about how funny it was to him that furnishing a home is apparently one of the major joys of a woman's life. She predictably hit him on the arm after each jest.

They made their way through nearly every aisle in the store, picking out their bedroom furniture and their dining room furniture along the way. Sovannah was writing down all the model numbers on a tiny little notebook that she pulled from her yellow purse. As they stopped at each item, Seth based all of his suggestions and agreements solely on the look that Sovannah had on her face as she studied at each one. Since he didn't care what pattern was on the legs of the dining room table, he might as well let her get what she wanted. They walked to the rug isle and he showed her the one with the intricate maze pattern. In the same manner that he used, she smiled and agreed on the rug mostly because he had picked it out.

After they chose their bedding and pillows, they took their long list of items to the sales desk at the back of the store, which Seth found interesting. "You ever wonder why furniture stores always seem backwards compared to other stores?"

"What do you mean?" Sovannah ripped out the two sheets full of model numbers from her little notebook and put the rest away inside her purse.

"I mean the clerks, the desks, the information booth, the place where you pay, it's all in the back usually. Everywhere else you pay right before you leave, but here, the only things near the doors are couches and paintings. Seems strange to me."

"Hmmm, you're right. Guess I've never noticed it before now." Sovannah said as she glanced around her. Seth was grateful that she seemed impressed by how he noticed things that everyone else simply took for granted. He always has some weird fact or new observation for her. Like how we drive on the parkway but park in the driveway, or how women blink twice as much as men, or how the longest word you can type on one row of a typewriter is "typewriter" or her favorite: that dolphins are the only other animal on the planet that has sex for pleasure. She was still skeptical about that one.

When they got to the counter, she spoke to the sales clerk as Seth simply stared at her and seemed to zone out. After a minute or so, she pulled a set of keys from her purse and handed them to him. "I'll fill out the paperwork and arrange for delivery, can you bring your car up front and start loading the smaller stuff? The guy is bringing some of it to the front."

"Sure." Seth took the keys and headed for the glass doors at the front, trying to avoid the overly peppy clerk Kelsey this time around. The sun was nearly set, and the sky was mostly black now with only a faint hue of blue. The parking lot lights were on, and as he stepped outside, he realized he had no idea what vehicle among the mass was his. He looked down at the keys and saw the "Ford" logo on the remote. He looked out into the parking lot and began pressing the lock button over and over, listening for a reaction. To his left, somewhere near the bookstore, he heard a horn beeping with each press of the button. He walked to that aisle and saw the taillights of a black SUV blinking. He walked over to it. *Ford Expedition XLT. Black with silver trim... 22" chrome rims... nice work, Seth.* He opened the door and hopped in with a prideful smile on his face. *And leather seats!*

He drove over to the front door and parked, where a large man in dungarees was waiting with a metal cart filled with various items. Seth hopped out and went around back, where he awkwardly fumbled with the rear door and lock as if he had never opened it before, as the man watched curiously.

After finally opening it and figuring out together how to lower the back row of seats, they loaded the rug, the blankets, the sheets, the pillows, the comforter, and a small wine rack into the back. The rolled-up rug reached all the way to the dashboard between the two front seats and the back door just barely closed.

They finished up and Seth thanked the man for his help just as Sovannah was exiting the store. "All done?"

"Yep. And still room for you and me." Sovannah reached for the passenger door and Seth quickly realized that he would have no sense of direction if he drove. "Hey, do you want to drive?"

She stopped in her tracks immediately. "You never want me to drive the Boss!" Sovannah had a suspicious look in her eye.

"Well, I figure since today is a special occasion and all...I'd..."

"Say no more." Before he even finished his sentence, Sovannah snatched the keys from him and walked around to the driver door and got in. "I don't want you to change your mind." Seth simply smiled and opened the passenger door. *That was easy.*

"Now maybe I can finally find out what the big deal is about this car."

"It's not a car you know, it is an SUV. Or you can call it a truck, but it's definitely not a car." Seth poked fun at her like he seemed to enjoy whenever she said something wrong.

"Whatever. Who names their vehicles anyways? The Boss! You're such a dork." She enjoyed any chance to turn the tables and make fun of him in return. His only reaction was to reach over and tickle her until they were both laughing.

After they settled down, they headed towards the condo as Seth eagerly watched out the window like an adventurer discovering new lands. He watched buildings he had never seen before come into view and then pass by just as quickly, out of sight and out of mind. He watched all the people on their way to some place to do something, and tried to imagine what each was thinking, and what each of their lives was like. Occasionally, he would pick a person at random and then try to imagine a life for them based solely on their appearance. He pictured their house, their car, their job, and wondered if they were married or had kids or pets. He imagined a past for them, and sometimes a future. He felt like an artist painting images of someone's life, or like a novelist, filling blank pages with the actions and experiences of another, creating a life for them as he went along. He wondered if the images he was creating in his mind for these people and of their futures were better than their actual lives. And sometimes he would see a homeless person and envision them stumbling upon a fortune in a dark alley, or a winning lottery ticket that would lift them from their emptiness into a better life. He enjoyed the idea of changing their lives, of rewriting their future, if only in his mind.

"Are you all right? You seem awfully quiet over there. What are you daydreaming about now?" He thought that Sovannah had an uncanny ability to tell when his mind was elsewhere.

"Just people watching. Wondering where everyone is going. What they are doing."

"The lady said the delivery truck should be there around 7:30 with the rest of the furniture. I know it's late, but we don't have to work tomorrow, so we can stay up all night setting it all up!" Seth could hear the excitement in her voice. "Plus, that gives us over an hour to get some food. Still want Chinese?"

"Sounds great. I am really hungry for some reason. I could go for some General Tso's Chicken!"

"Cashew chicken for me! And some egg drop soup! And Crab Rangoon!" Sovannah turned the truck off the main road. They passed a park on Seth's side of the vehicle, and he read the words on the large wooden sign as they passed, lit up by spotlights on either side. *Deer Park.* A silhouette of a deer with large antlers was carved into the wood and painted black. The sun was down, but bright lights still lit most of the park, and Seth could see several people on the various courts playing tennis or basketball. Others were jogging in their stretchy running gear with headphones in their ears, or similarly walking their dogs. Immediately after the park, they turned into an apartment complex.

"It's going to be nice living so close to the park!"

Seth nodded in agreement as he stared at the sign welcoming them to the complex. *Sonho Suites.* The main entrance was lined by large trees and lit by old fashioned looking street lanterns. Smaller streets branched off in either direction as they made their way to the very last set of buildings, which were more like condominiums than apartments. Each building was simply a large single story house that was divided into two separate apartments with their own garages and driveways. The outside of each building was lit with small lights that lined the perimeter and also the sidewalk leading up to the main door. The outer walls were covered halfway in multi-colored rock and the rest of the way in beige siding. The rocks were all various shades of brown and seemed to reach up from the ground, wrap around the building, and stretch high above to the chimney. The place was immaculately kept, and seeing the chimney, Seth realized each apartment must have a chimney.

"The fireplace will be nice this winter, too."

"I know. I can't wait! We can put the big round chair in front of it!" Sovannah pulled up to the last building and parked, turning towards Seth. "I wanted to say thanks for letting me go on a shopping spree back there. I know we talked about getting all new stuff for our new place together, and I know I went overboard a little. So thanks for not freaking out."

"No worries, you just won't get any Christmas presents or birthday presents for about three years, that's all." He cracked a smile at himself, reveling in his own joke.

She playfully stuck her tongue out at him and handed him the keys, poking fun at him one last time about naming his truck, and making air quotes with her fingers as she said the name. Seth smiled and walked to the door ahead of her, allowing him time to find the right key. He opened the door for her as she walked up, and then followed her inside.

The apartment was very spacious, and appeared even larger without any furniture. The floor plan was very open and the rooms all seemed to flow together. A couple of white pillars stretching from floor to ceiling separated the dining room from the living room, and likewise the kitchen was set apart by a long counter top bar. The flooring also helped to separate the areas, as it changed depending on the room. The kitchen and dining room were both hardwood, while the living room was carpeted. The line between the two types of flooring followed an arc, and the colors of the room matched those on the outside of the building. The appliances in the kitchen were all stainless steel, and the counter tops were marble, at least in appearance, giving the whole apartment a blended look of rustic and a modern at the same time. Across the room, Seth could see large glass doors that led to a cozy wooden deck extending off the back of the living room, facing a line of trees that joined those at the park nearby.

Sovannah sat her purse on the counter and did a little twirl across the dining room out into the living room where she bounced up and down while twirling in circles. She giggled and smiled with a childlike sense of happiness, and Seth just watched in adoration and amazement, as she danced. He dropped the keys on the counter and took a few elegant steps onto the hardwood where the dining table would eventually be placed. He held out the palm of his right hand towards her with a slight bow and spoke in his best gentleman voice. "May I have this dance, madam?"

She smiled and happily played along. "But of course, good sir." She stepped towards him and gently placed her fingers in his palm, offering a little curtsey of her own to this little fantasy.

He pulled her closer to him and looked her in the eye. "I must say 'tis Lovely out this evening, wouldn't you say?"

"A fine day indeed. May I ask what manner of business brings you here on this evening?"

"I come not on business matters madam, but pleasure. You see, I am but a lonely business man who seeks the companionship of a beautiful young lass. My fortune is without heir and my heart longs to find a suitable lady to spend my days with."

"I may be able to help you on this most endearing mission sir. What are your requirements for this young lady?"

Seth couldn't keep from grinning, but gathered himself before continuing. "This exceptional lass must have such beauty that she glows before my very eyes. Her hair must glisten with the color of rich walnut or mahogany as yours does, and her skin, much like yours, must be as soft as silky sheets. She must be roughly two to four inches shorter than myself so that when dancing we appear perfectly matched, as you and I are now."

Sovannah looked up at him. "I must say this girl you have described sounds too near to perfection to be real, yet I fear you limit her by comparing her to myself."

"I assure you, she is very real."

"And how will you know when you have found this girl?"

"I believe when our hands meet she will be filled with the same feelings that I have, and will be overcome by an urge to kiss me. That kiss shall end my search, and in her presence, I will be home."

Sovannah slowed her dancing down to a gentle sway and reached up her hands to pull Seth's lips closer. She put her lips on his and held them together for a few seconds before parting. "Welcome home."

Seth looked at her with Loving eyes. "Just so you know, you really are so close to perfect that I wonder if you could be real sometimes."

"Thanks." She smiled really big and let go of him, walking to her purse on the counter. "Now let's order some food. I'm starving." She picked up her phone and found the number for the Chinese place. "Still want General Tso's Chicken?"

"Yeah, and don't forget the Crab Rangoon."

Sovannah dialed the number as Seth walked to the glass doors on the other side of the room. He looked out onto the wooden deck and tried to picture cookouts and summer nights watching the sun go down behind the trees with her.

"Could you start bringing in the stuff in the car?" Sovannah asked as she waited for someone to pick up at the restaurant. Seth nodded his head and grabbed the keys on the way outside to the car. He stepped outside and took a deep breath. The air was fresh and cool. It was nearly seven o'clock and the light was beginning to fade. He stood outside for several minutes, just taking in the scenery, listening to the birds settle in for the night, fighting over the best spots. He pulled the rug, the blankets, the sheets, the pillows, the comforter, and a small wine rack out of the car. It was cooling down outside, and in two trips he carried everything to the door. When he opened it, Sovannah was just meeting him there, with an obvious look of disgust on her face.

"What's wrong?"

"Guess who called and left a message while I was ordering the food?"

Seth didn't even offer a guess before she continued again.

"The furniture people. Their stinkin' truck broke down and they can't deliver the rest of our stuff until the morning! We have nothing for tonight."

Seth looked down at the blankets and pillows he was holding. "At least we have these." Seth flashed a smile and they carried the stuff from the car into the living room and dropped it on the floor. "It will be all right, I promise. We can just have a little picnic on the floor. It will be fun."

His attitude about the whole thing lifted her spirits a little. "Okay, I suppose I'll try to go with the flow like you."

Seth smirked and said one of his quotes he was known for. "I don't just go with the flow baby, I AM the flow."

"You're such a dork."

They laid the rug on the carpet and covered it with the sheets, blankets, pillows and comforter, making a little bed in the middle of the floor in front of the fireplace. Seth walked over to the fireplace and looked for a way to turn it on. "It will get a bit chilly tonight lying on the floor, so I figure we could fire this baby up, what do you say?"

Sovannah finished arranging the linens and laid her head back on one of the pillows. "Sounds great."

Seth fiddled with the fireplace for a few more minutes before finally figuring out how a gas fireplace works. Just as the fire kicked on, the doorbell rang, startling him. He walked to the door and looked out the window. "Wow, the food is here already, that was quick. They must be close by. Where did you order from?"

"Yen Ching," she said. "My favorite." Sovannah sat up and placed the wine rack on its front in the middle of the picnic area to use as a little table. "It's only just down the road a ways."

Seth turned to her before opening the door. "What was the total?"

"I think it was twenty-one something."

He opened the door, and felt his back pocket, finding his wallet. He took out some cash and handed the money over, taking the food at the same time. "Thanks man, keep the change."

He shut the door and carried the bag over to Sovannah and set it on the wine rack. As they unwrapped their food and started eating, Seth could only look at Sovannah and smile. She was the perfect girl to him. Sweet, yet sassy. Honest and kind, yet fun. Beautiful, yet warm and approachable. *She's even beautiful when she eats.*

"I Looove Cashew Chicken!" She grinned from ear to ear.

Seth smiled at her and noticed she was more like him each time he was with her. "Try some of the Crab Rangoon, it is delicious. And I like when they fold the four corners of the pastry part up like these, and not in weird shapes like I've seen before. For some reason it seems better this way." Sovannah smiled at how he noticed the details in everything.

After they finished eating, Seth moved the wine rack to the side and laid his head on a pillow as she began picking up the trash and taking it all to the kitchen. The receipt fell from one of the bags and landed on the floor near Seth. He picked it up and noticed the date printed at the top. His eyes widened when he realized how old he was. *Thirty-two! Four more years!* To Seth, thirty always seemed so old, like a dividing line age between youth and the rest of life, and in just a few days he was already past it. He remembered the first time he saw Sovannah's beautiful face on that warm summer day in college. Yet in a few blinks of an eye, ten years had got behind him.

The gravity of it all sunk in to him, and for the first time since he found himself standing alone inside the furniture store, he thought about the beach. He shivered as he thought of the cold colorless sand, the ominous sky, and the dark, motionless water. He thought about the beach house, and each of his past encounters with it. He felt the emptiness of that place, and the hopelessness that it seemed to force upon him.

Sovannah finished in the kitchen and came back to him, although Seth barely noticed. He was lost in thoughts of broken boards, jagged glass, dust and darkness. "We forgot our fortune cookies!" Her delighted tone sort of snapped him back to this place. "Which one do you want?"

"You pick and just give me the other one. I will leave my fate in your hands."

She tossed him one and slid in next to him on the makeshift bed, laying her head on his shoulder and soaking up the heat from the fireplace. She cracked her cookie open, pulled out the little paper inside, and read it aloud.

"Whether you think you can or you think you can't, you are correct."

Seth nodded in agreement. "I like that one. Usually they are pointless but that one is actually a good quote. And no it doesn't mean you are always right."

Sovannah playfully smacked his arm. "Neither are you."

Seth opened his cookie. "My turn." He stares at it for several seconds before reading it to her. "Turning dreams into reality requires only waking." The words seemed to mock him. *If only...*

Sovannah closed her eyes and pressed her head into Seth's chest. "I could go for a dream right now. I need a nap." Seth ran his fingers through her hair and watched her chest rise and fall with each breath as he thought about his fortune. *If this is a dream, I don't want to wake up.* He thought about the other times he was with Sovannah, first at college, then on the ship, and now. He remembered holding her hand on the grass as they looked up at the stars the first time they met. He closed his eyes and remembered how the warmth of that moment faded to the cold of the beach. He felt the hot water of the hot tub on the deck of the ship as he held Sovannah close, her wet skin pressing against his. He remembered that moment too slipping away into the cold sand of the beach. *And now I'm here. Thirty-two years old. Holding her again.* He felt fear creep into his mind and crawl under his skin. He knew it might happen again. *Not this time... Please... I don't want to lose her. Just let me stay...*

Seth listened to her breaths and felt the warmth of the fire on his side. Outside the window he saw only complete darkness now. He rubbed her arm and smelled her hair, and tried to soak up every part of her in case it ended. Sovannah drifted off to sleep and he felt her muscles relax. She was sunk into him and he lay there motionless as to not disturb her. With every passing minute his relaxation grew, and her sleepiness seemed to crawl over to him. His body and mind struggled to stay awake. *Not yet... just stay awake... a little longer.*

He could feel her heartbeat and his own, beating in perfect rhythm as if with one heart. He felt the warmth of her body… the scent of her hair… the softness of her breath… his eyes closed and he held her… living only in the present… engulfed in the now.

CHAPTER THIRTEEN

WASHING STATION

11:32 p.m.
Sept. 6th, 2002
Liberum Medical Center
Springfield, IL

 It had been over an hour in the waiting room since the doctor left them, and most of it had been spent in silence. No other families or medical staff had even stopped by the room. Even the children, quick to bore and even quicker to pester one another, had managed to sit most of the time. The occasional trip to the bathroom or to make a purchase from the vending machines broke the monotony, and each member of the family welcomed these small moments of interaction or trivial noise. It was a relief, if only for a second, when they could let their mind think about something else. Anything but the possibility of losing a son, or a brother, or an uncle.

Charlie, trying to break the tension that blanketed the room, stood up and walked over to the box of the boy's belongings. He picked it up and carried it over to Gail, and set it on the floor at her feet. "I had forgotten until now, but this box has all the stuff they found in your son's car. The police dropped it off about an hour ago. I was keeping an eye on it until you all arrived."

Gail spoke somewhat clearly for the first time since arriving at the hospital. "Thanks, Charlie. You've been real good to my boy. I appreciate it."

Charlie smiled and nodded and sat back down, this time in the chair directly across from Gail and Arthur.

"You know, he is really lucky to have a family that cares for him so much."

Gail wiped a tear that was creeping down her cheek. "I just can't wait until he wakes up so I can tell him I Love him again."

Charlie knew the feeling well. "I'm sure he knows. And you all being here for him when he wakes up will make him feel a lot better."

Michelle scooted over a seat to join the conversation. "My brother is the only one of us who moved away from home, but we've always been a close family. A few hours isn't going to change that."

"Well, it will make everything he's going through that much easier for him."

"I can't imagine someone having to go through this all alone. Or why anyone wouldn't be there for their family?"

Michelle's words stung when Charlie heard them, and his eyes slammed shut. It was like a hot knife shot right through his skin and hit him in the stomach. Charlie knew she meant no harm and had no idea about his past, but he couldn't help feeling the sharpness of those words, and the painful memories they stirred. He took a deep breath and opened his eyes, trying, but failing to keep them dry.

Charlie could tell that Michelle and Gail noticed the change in his face. He could see in their faces, that they knew they struck a nerve. He dropped his eyes to the floor, and several seconds passed before he spoke.

"I'm sorry. I just..."

Michelle leaned in a little closer to Charlie, who couldn't get the sentence out. "Are you all right? Was it something I said? I'm sorry if..."

"Oh no, don't worry about it. I... I have my own problems I guess. And you guys don't need me adding anything else negative to this night."

Gail, whose motherly instincts were already revved up, jumped at the chance to make someone feel better.

"It's okay, Charlie. We are friends now, and you can tell us whatever you need to."

Charlie stared at the floor for a few more seconds before continuing.

"It was about seven months ago. My boy was in a car wreck too. His name was Michael and he would have been twenty-two this fall."

Michelle's eyes widened when she heard him say those words. "*Would* have been..."

"They brought him to this very same hospital."

"I'm so sorry, Charlie."

"Me too. I've told him a hundred times since that night. I don't know if he can hear me, but if so, I just hope he can forgive me."

"Of course he forgives you."

"I hope so, but I can't seem to forgive myself."

Charlie's words were quiet and somber, and the room was silent. Even the vending machines seemed to quiet down as he spoke. "I decided to work late that night. I missed his call asking for a ride home. So he drove himself, even though he had a few beers. By the time I got the news and rushed over here, he was already gone. It was here in the hospital that I first heard the message he left me on my phone. The words hurt each time I listen to it, but I suffer just to hear his voice once more. If I could do one day over again in my life, that would be the day I would choose. Even if I couldn't change what happened, I just wish I could have been there to say goodbye to him. He deserved that at least."

Charlie still stared at the floor and took a few deep breaths while everyone focused on him. He reached his hand in his pocket and put his hand on his cell phone. He rubbed it with his thumb as he spoke.

"The last thing he said to me in his voicemail was 'I'll see ya when I see ya.' That was one of his catchphrases. He used to say that every time he left the house, and at the end of phone conversations."

A tear left his eye and it was so quiet you could almost hear it hit the tile between his shoes. The silence was broken after a few seconds by the sound of Michelle sobbing uncontrollably.

Charlie looked up at her. "Oh, I'm sorry. I knew I shouldn't have said anything. You guys don't need this story on a night like tonight."

Michelle put her hand over her eyes and spoke erratically through her sniffles. "It's fine. I... I was just trying to think of the last thing that my brother said to me, and I can't remember."

Brian rubbed her shoulders. "Don't worry about it. You will talk to him again really soon." He pulled a tissue from the box on the table next to him and handed it to her.

She wiped her eyes with it, smearing her mascara. "I know. I keep thinking about a conversation we had a few weeks ago over the phone. He always talked about meeting this perfect girl. The girl of his dreams. He has described her to me a hundred times, and I'm just afraid. What if he never gets a chance to meet her? What if he never falls in Love? What if..."

Brian cut her off and handed her another tissue. "You can't think like that. Don't do that to yourself. Just keep being positive."

She leaned in and put her head on Brian's shoulder. The room stayed silent for a couple of minutes, until she gathered herself and wiped her eyes. She sat up and looked at Charlie again. "I'm real sorry about Michael too, Charlie. I'm sure he knows you care about him." She motioned over to the other side of the room. "You know, my son Marcus' middle name is Michael too."

Charlie looked over at the kid, who was pointing out the window with Mariah. "Good looking young boy."

"He's named after his uncle, who's middle name is also Michael."

Charlie just shook his head. *"What are the odds...?"*

The motherly tone returned to Michelle's voice. "If being here with all of us, and my brother's accident, are too rough on you, I understand if you want to go home Charlie. You have done a lot, and we are grateful, but if you need to take off, we get it. Don't feel like you need to stay around here for us."

Charlie still held his cell phone tight in his right hand in his pocket. "It's ok, I..."

Just as he was starting his sentence, the door quickly opened. The same doctor walked in holding a folder open in front of him, staring at the pages. He walked up to them and snapped it shut before looking up at them.

Ryan and Rachel, who were resting their eyes, seated against the back wall, immediately stood and walked over to the rest of the group. Gail spoke before the doctor got a word out. "Dr. Kaplan. Tell me you have good news about my boy."

The doctor looked straight at her. "Well, the surgery is complete, and we had no serious complications. We have no reason to believe at this time that he won't make a full recovery."

A few people in the room let out a sigh of relief.

"However, and I can't stress this enough; I can't promise you anything just yet. We've seen both good and bad outcomes from injuries like the one he sustained tonight, and as of now, he is currently sedated in a medically induced coma."

"When can we talk to him?"

"Not yet. We will likely keep him unconscious for twenty-four to forty-eight hours while we monitor his vitals and keep a close eye on his brain activity. After that, we will dial back the medicine and hopefully his body will begin to support itself and gain consciousness within the first few hours."

Ryan was quick to point out the most critical word in the doctor's sentence. "Hopefully?"

"Like I said, there are no guarantees. Every patient is different. Every injury is different. Every brain is affected differently. We've called for the head neurologist in the area, and he should be here in the morning to do a full assessment of his brain scans and responses. As of this time, we've done all we can do here and we are confident. But from this point forward, it will be up to his body to recover... and fate, if you will. All you can do is wait at this point."

"Can we see him at least? I can't take any more of this room."

"Absolutely. Having family there would be good for him too." Once again, the words stung as Charlie heard them. The doctor stood up and peeked inside the folder one last time. "If you would all like to follow me, I'll take you to his recovery room."

Those who were still sitting all stood up nearly in unison. Gail turned to Charlie as they stepped towards the door behind the doctor. "I'd like it if you stayed Charlie. My boy will want to meet you." Charlie simply nodded and filed in line with the others.

Michelle immediately regained her composure and spoke with authority again. "Mom, you and Dad go ahead." She turned to the back of the room. "Kids, get over here. We are going to see your uncle now. Just be quiet and follow us. No horsing around."

They all headed down the hall, passing through a door that required a code to be entered before entry was granted, and then through a few more turns before the doctor finally stopped at a large door and waited for the group to gather around.

"Now on the other side of this door, there is a washing station. You all will be required to wash your hands and put on a paper gown over your clothes before proceeding through the following door. We have some burn patients in this ward as well, and they are very susceptible to bacteria and contaminants."

He noticed that Marcus was holding a pop can in his hand. "And you will not be allowed to take any food or beverages past this point. I'm sorry." Marcus tossed the nearly empty can into the trashcan outside the door.

The doctor opened the door to the ward and each family member in turn washed their hands and put on a paper gown, helping each other tie them in the back. Once they were all finished, he led them to one of the rooms. The curtain was half drawn and they could see only his feet through the glass doors. As the doctor stepped over the threshold, the automatic sliding glass door opened and he stepped through.

It was a small room and they crowded in, slowly forming a semi-circle about three feet around the patient's bed. He was laying there motionless, with several tubes and sensors attached to him. His head was shaved and nearly half of it was covered in bandages and gauze. There was a large tube coming out of his throat, and the ends of a machine were attached to his nose with smaller tubes inserted. Various beeps and oxygen machines could be heard.

Almost on sight of him, crying filled the room. Up to now it somehow felt like a bad dream for most of them, but seeing him was like waking from that bad dream and learning it wasn't a dream at all. Reality set it and the shock of it all became very real for all of them.

The doctor walked over to check the monitors and machines while each member of the family took turns venturing up close to the bed near his head. There was not a dry eye in the room. Gail and Arthur walked up first, and Gail pressed tightly against him, covering her eyes with his shoulder. "Our poor boy..." Those were the only words she managed before being overwhelmed by sobbing. Michelle was on the other side and held her brother's hand the whole time as the rest of the group came closer too.

Gail kissed him on the forehead and Arthur simply patted him on the head without saying a word. He strained to maintain his stoic strength in front of his family.

The children seemed scared to go near him at all, and Mariah simply hid behind her father's legs and cried.

Michelle looked over at Charlie. "Come on, Charlie. I

know you've met him, but I'm sure he'd be glad to know you are here too."

Charlie stepped a little closer. "He looks so different with his head shaved and all those things attached to him."

Michelle continued rubbing his lifeless hand. "We're all here for you, buddy."

They all just watched him lay there for a few very long minutes, listening to the beeps of the machines and watching the oxygen device pump air into his lungs and then out again a second later. He was lifeless except for the rise and fall of his chest, which gave them hope, even if it was mechanically produced. They watched almost in hypnosis as the constant drip of the IV machine fed chemicals into his body.

Dr. Kaplan, speaking directly to Gail and Arthur, broke the tranquility. "I know this probably isn't something you want to think about right now, but I have to ask. Do you know what your son's wishes are about being kept alive artificially?"

Gail looked up at him with wet eyes, managing only a single word. "Artificially?"

"Yes. It is a very real possibility that when we ease him off the anesthetic, his body might fail to control his needs. Basically, if his body is unable to sustain life on its own, we would use machines to simulate breathing and the beating of his heart. He would be alive in the technical sense, but without consciousness, unable to survive without the machines. Some people would prefer not to live this way. Did you ever speak to him about this?"

"No. He's twenty-two. Of course not." Loud sniffles and crying from nearly everyone in the room accompanied the doctor's words.

"Okay, it's not something that needs to be decided right now, and I hope it doesn't come to that, but I just want you to be aware that there is still a possibility that a decision will have to be made in that regard." This time Gail could only manage a nod of her head. Michelle squeezed his hand even harder.

"Now, since your son is over eighteen years old, it's technically his decision, but if he is unable to give it, and you do not know his wishes on the matter, the decision in that case would be left to the parents."

Michelle, unable to control herself anymore, let go of her brother's hand and walked to the door. She stepped outside the room into the hallway and covered her mouth, trying to keep the sobbing down so the nurses and other people couldn't hear.

"I'm sorry to make you think about these things. But I have to do my job, and I just need you to be prepared for everything just in case. Now do you have any questions for me?"

Everyone just stared at him silently or nodded their head. Michelle could be heard sobbing loudly outside the room, unable to control it. Brian was preoccupied with Marcus and Mariah, so Charlie stepped out to see if she was ok.

"Okay, then. There are no specific visitor hours in this ward, so feel free to stay by his side as long as you like. I'll be leaving for now, but I'll be back tomorrow. We should know more when the neurologist gets here. He should be here in the morning."

Dr. Kaplan left the room and Gail reached down and held Seth's hand. "Hang in there bud. You hear me? Hang in there for Mom."

CHAPTER FOURTEEN

EMPTY BOXES

Seth didn't need to open his eyes to know. He felt the change in the air. His nap with Sovannah in their makeshift bed in front of the warm glow of the fire, was over. Whether it ended minutes ago, or days, or years, didn't matter to him. Time didn't make sense anymore. He knew she was gone again. Under him he still felt the rug, and could smell the familiar scent of dust and age in the air. Yes, the beach had brought him back again.

He opened his eyes and looked around him. It was much the same as before, as if he hadn't moved since the last time he found himself upon this rug, hand bloodied and dripping onto the intricate maze pattern beneath. The colors of the rug stood out among the gray dullness that filled the room. It was brilliant and bright, seemingly new, just as it was that warm day in the furniture store. He rubbed his fingers along the soft fibers, plush and silky to the touch.

The wound, which was wet and aching just before he closed his eyes, was now a scar when he opened them… dry, cracked, and aged in the blink of an eye. Seth might have considered this impossible, but this place seemed to blur the lines between possible and impossible, real and unreal, dreams and reality. He rubbed his thumb along the raised skin of the scar, tracing the edges where the glass from the mirror penetrated his skin only moments ago. He looked down at the colorful rug, and lost himself in the maze once again.

If there was any sliver of hope in him that these glimpses into the future with Sovannah were just illusions, just dreams behind his closed eyes, this scar seemed to offer proof otherwise. To him, only a few moments had passed since he smashed his hand into the mirror, enough time for a nap at most. Yet on the other side of that nap was a scar that screamed of time gone by. Years were passing in the blink of an eye with each wonderful illusion of her. Lost years, that he never got to experience, that would never get back. That he would never have in the first place. *But why? Why me? Why all of this?*

On the rug, next to him was a small rectangular piece of paper with writing on it. He picked it up and raised it to his face. It was old but still readable, though the words were small and some letters were rubbed dull. He read the words in his head. *"Turning one's dreams into reality requires simply waking."*

The words were haunting, and he thought about the first time he read them aloud to Sovannah. They seemed to carry new meaning now. It seemed so simple. It was all he wanted in one sentence. To wake and be with her. Or to fall asleep and be with her. He wasn't sure which.

Seth closed his eyes and begged to wake up. He wanted this to end. That the dark beach and this beach house would vanish. That his illusions of Sovannah were not only real, but just on the other side of his closed eyes. He opened them, only to be greeted by the dusty gray boards of the floor and the cracked walls across the room. He closed them again, as tears began to form in the corners of his eyes. *Why are you doing this to me? What is the point of all of this?* He didn't even know where he was directing the words, or to whom he might be asking the questions. He asked anyway, hoping to get answers.

He raised his eyes and looked above him. He often struggled with the idea of faith, and his mind always juggled the possibilities in his head. It was only when he was out in nature among the trees and animals, that he could convince himself of the presence of a higher power, and to a greater extent, an inner power. Yet his questions, fears, and doubts never went away.

"Why?" he spoke the words quietly into the silence of the room as his hand balled into a fist.

"Why!!" he cried louder, raising his hand.

"Why!!!" he screamed and slammed his fist into the carpet under him. The tears fell as he pounded his fist into the rug over and over. His face was red and his fist began to ache. A glimmer caught his eye and he stopped to stare at his fist, seemingly enjoying the painful throb of each heartbeat. A shine grabbed his attention from a ring on his third finger. *The ring...*

When he saw it, his anger grew. *What good is it?* He stood, stuffed the fortune in his pocket, and walked back through the house to doorway, each step full of confused anger. He stepped through the opening where the door used to be, and looked up at the stars outside.

"What is this place!?" He spoke loudly and powerfully. He paced back and forth on the wooden porch, kicking a broken piece of wood from the door. "Hello!?" There was nothing but silence. He picked up a larger piece of wood and swung it at the hanging glass that was the remains of the window, shattering it and sending it flying inside the house. He swung the board like a baseball bat at the brittle railing over and over, breaking it in several places, before throwing it out onto the sand in disgust. He stood there with his head in his hands, sobbing. His hands ached from clinching the wood so fiercely.

Slowly, hanging his head in defeat, he walked after the piece of wood out onto the beach. He stopped and just stared at the wood without picking it up. The outburst had been cathartic, and helped to calm his anger. He simply turned his eyes to the water. His thoughts raced under the bright light of the moon and stars above. He looked at his hand again, watching the light of the moon bounce off the edges of the ring. *I don't remember asking... I don't remember a wedding... I don't remember any of it.* With his thumb he spun the ring in circles around his finger, watching it spin. *So what's the point?* He was torn between a body that has aged ten years in a few blinks of the eye, and a mind that felt as if it was in college merely hours ago. In between were a few scattered memories with Sovannah that both felt out of place. *I'm living my life in pieces... in broken dreams...*

He pulled the fortune from his pocket and read the last two words again. "...simply waking." *But which is the dream...*

"Am I dreaming at all?" He looked around him again. A single thought came to him that struck him with fear. *What if I'm dead? Maybe that is the answer I've been looking for. Maybe that's the reason for all of this...* He raised his eyes to the stars and spoke aloud, hoping to find solace in his own voice. Yet even his voice seemed distant and unfamiliar to him. "Am I dead?" There was no answer. He looked at the beach house. His voice left him. He could only mouth the words. *"Is this hell?"*

He stood there, staring at the beach house in total silence, motionless, lost in the horrible idea that maybe this wasn't a dream at all. That this was his reality, a reality he could never wake up from. Fittingly, the words to one of his favorite poems that he ever wrote crossed his mind. *"Maybe I have walked these very shores before, but never as it now had seemed. And maybe life and death are simply doors, among the many hallways I have dreamed."*

His eyes were focused on the beach house. He took a step towards it but stopped. *I... I can't go in...* He was torn between desire and fear. He knew what going back inside could mean. Another wonderful, yet fleeting glimpse of a life with Sovannah. Another day in the perfect Eden of her existence. Another dip in the sublime sea of their life together.

But it could also mean something else. Another pain-filled departure. Another torturous, yet futile struggle to hold onto the dream. Another startling and defeating return to this desolate place. Another undetermined period of time that would be lost to him forever. A gaping hole in his mind. A forgotten piece of himself.

He looked down at the ring again and thought about what might be waiting for him. There was no way for him to know what kind of future he might be jumping into. *Maybe Sovannah won't be there... Maybe another ten years has gone by, and something has happened to her... or to us... What if she's dead... what if we are no longer together?*

The possibilities flew in and out of his mind one after another, but his thoughts kept landing on one single thought and one single image. *Her eyes. Her perfect, mesmerizing, infinite eyes...* He closed his own eyes and pictured the way hers lit up when she smiled, or drifted off when she was in thought. He remembered how helpless he was when she looked at him, how weak he felt inside. When he opened his eyes, he realized that without knowing it, he had taken several steps towards the beach house. This seemed to make his mind up for him. *One more glimpse of her... one more kiss... I don't care what I find there. I don't care what it takes. I will take that chance.*

    He walked up the broken steps and back into the beach house. It was the first time he went in actually determined to leave, determined to set off another dream. He walked through the kitchen and dining rooms, glancing around for something to grab his attention the way it had the first few times. Nothing stood out. He grabbed one of the boxes and pulled the folded flaps to open it. It was empty. He grabbed another and did the same. *Empty?* He walked around and kicked a few other boxes with his foot to feel for weight. They were all empty. *All of them? But I don't get it... Where did all the stuff go?*

    He walked rather hastily to one of the bedrooms and jerked open two drawers on one of the dressers, one with each hand. Inside were several stacks of neatly folded shirts and bottoms. He pulled open two more drawers, only to find more clothes, neatly folded and color arranged. The colors were bright and really stood out among the dullness that surrounded them. It was almost if they glowed in the bright light of their color. He ran his hand along the edges of the items, feeling the softness. He closed his eyes and hoped this would take him to Sovannah, much like the rug. He opened his eyes and he was still in the beach house. He turned and threw open the closet door. Inside were several three-button polo shirts and neatly hanging slacks. He stood there, bewildered by the site. *How did they get here? Who unpacked the boxes and put the clothes away organized and neat?*

Seth shut the door and walked back through the dining room into the kitchen. He stopped and looked all around him. Each cabinet door appeared brand new. The hinges and knobs were polished and shining. *I don't get it...* He opened some of the cabinets in confusion. Inside he saw the dishes, clean and new, stacked in sorted piles very neatly. *Who could have done this?* He opened several drawers in a fury, looking for something, but not knowing what. Some memory, some feeling, that could take him from this place. Anything that would take him back to Sovannah. Yet nothing seemed to catch his eye. *Come on... find something.* He opened the fridge and looked around. He slammed it shut. Nothing was working. He was growing impatient.

He walked outside onto the porch and looked up and down the beach. Silence and stillness was all he found. He looked up at the stars to catch his breath. *Now what?* He sat down sideways on the steps and closed his eyes to think about Sovannah. This is the one time he tried to go to her and couldn't. He looked down at the ring and spun it few times on his finger. *Maybe it's over. Maybe I can't get back to her again. Maybe I'm stuck here for good now.* He leaned his head against the rail and stared at the side of the beach house, feeling defeated and more alone than ever. A tear rolled down his face and fell onto the dry wood beneath, disappearing almost instantly. He blinked a few times and watched the moon glisten on his wet eyelashes.

With his head against the rail, he scanned the side of the wall and saw something he had never noticed before. On the weathered wood above the door, there seemed to be an outline of some numbers on the outside of the beach house. He could tell that at one time, numbers were hung or nailed into the wood, and the elements had worn the wood differently underneath, leaving it a different color. He wiped the tears from his eyes and looked a little harder. The outline clearly showed the numbers "9064" and on each outline there were tiny holes near the top and bottom where nails once were.

He looked below and around him but could see no trace of the numbers on the wooded deck or in the sand around it. His eyes turned to the water once again. He had barely looked at it since the time he swam out as far as he could. It seemed so long ago, yet so recent. He wasn't sure which he felt more. He was becoming disconnected with this place too. His thoughts bounced around in his head. *Maybe I've seen all I was supposed to see... Maybe there is no more... No more of her, no more of me... Then what does it all mean? What is next? Anything? Maybe this IS hell... Maybe that's what hell is... unanswered questions... unfulfilled dreams... endless confusion... endless want...*

Seth was feeling exhausted, emotionally and physically, and didn't want to think anymore. He looked to the sky and stared at the moon and stars. He closed his eyes and longed for the sun. A tear dribbled down his cheek...

CHAPTER FIFTEEN

STONE LIONS

    Seth's head was resting against the window. His eyes were shut, enjoying a nap, as the vibrations from the road filtered through to his body. Outside the car, the sun was low in the sky. As the trees zipped by in a line alongside the road, the sunlight blinked continuously on Seth's face, which bounced slightly with each undulation of the pavement beneath.
    A sizeable dip in the road caused his head to lift and fall back against the glass with a slight knock, rousing his senses from their slumber. His eyelids were heavy and reluctant to open. A tear had made its way to his lip, and he tasted the salt. The sound of the tires beating on the pavement provided a constant background noise to the rhythmic beat of the music coming from the speakers in the door and on the dash. He raised his hand to rub his eyes and speed up the waking

process.

"How was the nap?" Sovannah's voice pierced through the noise from his left. He pieced his surroundings together and raised his eyelids to look out the window. The blinking light from the sun streaming in from behind the trees caused him to squint until they adjusted. He saw the grass along the road fly by in a blur of green. A warmth fell over him knowing she was with him again. To see her again was all he wanted. One more day. One more glimpse. It was his only drive now, but it was destroying him at the same time. Years were passing in the blink of an eye. The joy of each day with her was starting to get weighed down by the thought of the thousands of days in between that he missed. And drifting away from her each time was more painful than the last.

"Hard to wake up from." He wanted to tell her what was happening to him. He wanted to explain. He wanted her to know everything, but he couldn't figure out how to do it. It never seemed like the time. And he didn't want to ruin the moments with her. So he just went along with each day, savoring the time, unable to bring it up. And it showed in his voice. "Feels like I've been asleep for years. How long was I out?"

"About two hours, I think."

Her voice sounded the same, but he was both nervous and anxious to turn his head and look at her. When he did, a smile flashed on his face. She was more beautiful than ever. Her skin was golden brown from the summer season. She was wearing a light and airy white summer top. A pink tank top could be seen beneath it, as well as tan lines on her shoulder. Her window was down slightly and her hair gently whipped in the wind behind her. She had large sunglasses on that covered her eyes, and she was smiling as she talked.

"I took over driving after we stopped for gas and

drinks. I think that was at like one thirty, what time is it now?"

Seth blocked the sun from the dash to better see the numbers. "Three twenty two." When he said the numbers he realized he had no idea how much time had passed since he was last with her. If any had passed at all, he couldn't tell from looking at her. He looked around and noticed a magazine lying in the back seat. As he reached for it, he saw there were a few bags and a suitcase in the backseat. *Where are we headed? Are we on another trip?* He put these thoughts aside for now and grabbed the magazine to inspect the cover. *July 2017. We are thirty-seven... It has been five more years...* He flipped down the visor above him to get a look at his face in the mirror. He seemed to notice the years more on his own face. More gray in the stubble on his chin and jaw line, more gray in his temples, the beginnings of wrinkles around his eyes.

Now that Seth was awake, Sovannah rolled the window up the rest of the way, and turned the music nearly all the way down, until the song was no longer discernible, and only a faint beat could be heard in the background. "We are getting closer. We should be there in less than an hour. I'm not sure how far it is, once we get off the main road. I still can't believe we are doing this, can you? I've never done anything so crazy… I'm not very spontaneous!"

Seth had no idea what she was talking about, and not knowing how to respond, was hoping this was a hypothetical question. Luckily, Sovannah continued, "These last four months have been such an emotional roller coaster."

Seth had many questions floating through his mind that he couldn't ask her. *What has happened? Where are we coming from? Where are we headed? Why are there packed bags in the back seat?* He did his best to answer her vaguely and keep her talking. "I know what you mean."

Sovannah reached over and grabbed his hand and

squeezed it. He saw the diamond shine in the sun. "Thanks for being so strong during my father's funeral. I'm not sure I could have made it through that day without you."

Seth's face went blank. He had no memory of her father, or his funeral. He simply squeezed her hand back and rubbed her fingers with his thumb. "You're welcome."

"I know he and I weren't close, but I guess I always thought there was a chance we could be someday."

"I'm sorry."

"It's okay. And I'm so glad you talked me into this. I can't wait to see the place. I've never been the adventurous type. I mean, who does this sort of thing anyways?"

"I'm not sure. I guess we do." *What adventure is she talking about? What place?*

"I think I'll miss everything. But I'm excited at the same time, you know?" Sovannah's voice changed in tone. "I mean, just think, a few months ago we are living in a small condo with bills and worries and complaining about our jobs. It was simple. It was safe. That's how I liked it. And look at us now. All that is gone. Would you have ever guessed that today we would be doing this? I've never quit my job before."

"No, it's pretty crazy I gue..."

"Oh, I just remembered!" Sovannah blurted the words out and interrupted him like she always did when something came to her all of a sudden. "Sorry, but the delivery guys called while you were asleep. They just delivered the rest of the boxes. So I guess our stuff beat us there. They asked if they could just pile the boxes outside the door on the patio and I said yes, since we would be there soon. Otherwise we would have to wait until Monday. I didn't want that to happen again. Remember that first night in our condo?"

Seth seemed to drift off a little when she mentioned the condo. "Yeah. One of the best days of my life was the day we moved in. I remember every detail of that first day… like it was yesterday." Seth hesitated saying the words. Yesterday seemed like a foreign concept to him. Days in general seemed meaningless. All of time seemed to exist for him in small moments. Past… present… future… today… yesterday… tomorrow… These were just words now. Words without meaning. The only time that existed for Seth anymore was… now.

"Every detail? Like what?" Sovannah was always amazed at the things Seth would remember.

"Everything. Driving up the road to it past the park. Opening the door for the first time. How empty everything looked. Planning where everything will go. Dancing in our future dining room. I even remember what we ate that night. Chinese. You had Cashew Chicken."

"I suppose you even know what was in your fortune cookie!" Seth didn't answer her. He simply smiled until she turned and looked at him. "You do? Seriously? No way."

Seth turned his head and looked out the window at the grass flying by next to the road and closed his eyes. The world went silent to him. The sun flickered through the trees onto his eyelids as he spoke. "Turning dreams into reality requires simply waking." After saying the words he took a deep breath and was scared to open his eyes. He was afraid she would be gone. Or he would be. Either way, he didn't want to leave her again. Not yet.

"Wow, how do you do that?" Her voice crashed through the silence again, just as when he woke in the car the first time. He opened his eyes and leaned over and kissed her.

"I don't know. I guess…" Seth paused for a second. "…to me it feels like it just happened. It feels so close. My brain is just weird like that I guess. I have no idea what it's doing half the time."

"Well, I like your weirdness." Sovannah gave Seth a playful smile. "It's cute. And fun. And I like it. And I like how adventurous you are. I mean, I probably wouldn't be doing this on a whim without you. I would have just put Dad's letter away after the first time I read it and went back to my boring life. I wouldn't have the courage to leave my job, sell my condo, pack my stuff, and just move ten hours away to some place I've never been. But you… without a care in the world you said 'Let's Go!' And here we are…"

Seth rubbed the inside of her thigh and gave it a little squeeze. "As long as I'm with you, I don't care where we go." He still had questions but didn't know how to ask them. So he improvised. "By the way, did you pack the letter? I wouldn't mind seeing it again."

"Yeah, it's in the glove compartment with the key and our other papers I think."

Seth opened the pull down door in front of him and found a folded up handwritten note that was clearly written a while ago. It was two pages long and a key was taped to it near the bottom of the second page. He read the words quietly to himself.

To my dearest Sovannah,

If you are reading this letter, it means my time here in this crazy world has finally expired. It also means that I have failed in my goal of re-connecting with you. As of this writing, I am gravely sick, and feel as if this is my final chance to tell you all that I have been thinking over the last couple of years. I know I've been out of touch, but if I beat this sickness I promise to meet you and tell you these things in person. If not, then I am very sorry you have to hear from me in a letter.

I know I haven't always been the greatest father, and I know we haven't been as close over the years as we both would have liked, but I swear to you no one feels worse about that than I do. I have failed you in many ways as a father, but I can only hope after I am gone that I might be able to make amends for it in some way. And maybe give you some advice so that you learn from my mistakes.

I spent my life following a career and money, and it was the greatest mistake of my life. It cost me the dreams I had as a young man, and also my family, and I would change it all if I could. I should have been there for your mother before she passed. I should have been there for you. I should have been there as you chased your own dreams.

Seth flipped the page and continued reading.

I know money controls many of our

actions, but I plan to help out in that regard. Perhaps this will help to make up for some of the pain I have caused you in my life.

I have instructed my lawyer to cash in my meager investments and give the money to you upon my death. I know this can't make up for all of our lost time, but hopefully it will afford you the freedom you need to live the life I wish I could go back and live.

So here is my advice and hope for you:
That you would follow your dreams at all costs.
That you would let your heart lead you places.
That you would live a better life than I did.

And what better place to start than the place I started so many years ago. My final gift to you is the key below and the life that it may bring. It belongs to the cottage where I met your mother so long ago. It belongs to the place where you were born, before we left for a richer life in a different place. It was left to me by my father, and now I leave it to you.

The land has been in our family for many years. I hung on to it, always hoping to one day return. It may need some TLC, but I hope you find it as glorious as I did. And I hope you use it to follow your passions and to find Love along the way. And if you do find it, Sovannah, hold onto it with everything you have, like I failed to do.

I'm sorry and I Love you,

Dad

Seth found many of the answers he was looking for. He sat there for a moment in thought before folding the paper up and placing it back in the glove compartment.

Sovannah was the first to break the silence. "I haven't seen the place in years. Not since I was a little girl. I barely remember it actually. I didn't even know he still owned it." Sovannah slowed down and made the turn off the highway onto a smaller, two-lane road.

"It sounds like a wonderful place." Seth looked around him but couldn't tell where they might be. "I'm guessing you know how to get there?" To Seth this was a reasonable question but she assumed he was picking on her as usual.

"I'm not an idiot. I can follow directions. Besides, I programmed it into my phone. See?" She showed him the screen on her phone, but all he could discern in the sunlight was a red dot right in the middle of the screen.

"Just checking. So what's the plan after we get there?"

"Well, I haven't really decided yet. I figured we could

just chill for a while, you know? I mean I know you said it would be dumb to take a few years off and just live off the money Dad gave us until it ran out, and I agree. We should do something better with it. But we don't have to decide right away."

Seth just listened, taking in everything she said, trying not to interrupt.

"I mean, we won't really have many bills, so we won't need that much income to sustain us. And I thought you had some really good ideas the other day."

Seth knew he would have to speak eventually. "I try my best."

"You were right when you said if we were going to do this, then we had to do it right. We had to do what the letter said. We had to take the leap fully. We had to follow our passions. You were right, as usual." Sovannah playfully smacked his arm. "And I can't wait to get back into painting. I don't know why I ever stopped. I guess life got in the way. But now I will finally be able to. And I think it's cool that you want to start writing a book. You've always talked about that. I think you will do great."

Seth just looked at the trees going by and wondered what he would write about.

"And eventually, maybe I will start a yoga class in town. That's probably my favorite of your ideas."

"Sovannah the yoga instructor… I like that." As Seth spoke, Sovannah slowed the car as they approached a narrow entryway into the trees on the right.

"I think this is it. That was quick. I guess we were closer than I thought."

Seth looked out the window. It wasn't much of a road at all. It was one lane, unpaved, and more like an overgrown four wheeler track than a driveway. It trailed away into the trees, bending out of sight.

"Yep, there are the lions. This is it." Sovannah had obvious excitement in her voice. Seth looked in front of him as they passed between the stone monuments. On either side of the entrance were two small concrete platforms upon which sat two stone lions at roughly eye level that stared out and appeared to guard the small trail. In Seth's mind, their faces snarled, and their eyes seemed to be staring at him intently, following him slightly as they moved.

"Those lions are pretty cool, but a little creepy. I guess whoever put them here wanted their privacy." They continued slowly down a curvy trail that veered back and forth and was lined with tall thin trees swaying at the tops in the breeze. The long trunks stretched up high above their car. The branches and leaves were far above them.

They continued on the trail, wheels turning slowly, hearts racing wildly, for what felt like ten minutes, before seeing a place ahead where the trees opened up a bit. As they approached, they could see that the trail ended in a small circular courtyard lined with a stone wall on the far half of the semi-circle. The tree line ended at the courtyard too. They stopped the car and stepped out without even shutting the doors. They stood in silence for a few seconds, taking in the scenery, and then made eye contact. Sovannah smiled and spoke with a child-like excitement. "We made it!"

Seth simply smiled back at her and looked up at the sun shining at an angle through the trees. He could hear the wind blowing the treetops back and forth, and could smell the wonderful scents that were somehow familiar to him. Off in the distance, he could hear the crashing of water slightly. *Water? Are we near the beach? Could this be...*

Across the courtyard was a gap in the stone wall. Upon either side were two more stone lions. They were smaller this time, and to Seth, appeared to be smiling slightly, almost welcoming him and Sovannah, unlike the ones at the other end of the lane. Seth could do nothing but smile back. "You are sure we are in the right place?" Although Seth felt a strange connection to this place, he felt the need to ask.

"Yep, I remember this stone wall. I remember walking along the top of it as a little girl. And I remember the lions!" As she said the words, she walked over to one of the lions guarding the gap in the stone wall and rubbed her hand along the nose.

"See, you remember things too. All the way back to when you were a little girl. I guess I'm not the only weird one. Our minds are capable of doing some amazing things." He could smell the hint of salt in the air, and he feared what it could mean. "You know, smell is the sense most closely linked to memories." He took a deep breath through his nose with his eyes shut.

She flashed her adorable smile at him. "We are definitely where we are supposed to be. I remember it all now. It's like a piece of my childhood has come back to me. I remember hopping on the stone steps that lead down from this rotunda to the cottage below. I remember jumping off the last step onto the sand as a kid. I remember running along the edge of the water trying to dodge the waves. Besides, the address is right. Look."

Sovannah pointed at the stone just below the lion to the left of the steps that led down to the bottom. Seth walked over to join her, and looked at the number carved into the stone just below the lion. He froze in his tracks. Time seemed to stop again. He could feel each beat of his heart thump in his ear. *9064. It can't be... It can't be the same...*

Sovannah hopped up onto the stone wall just as she did as a child. She looked over the edge, beyond where the trees stopped. Her eyes lit up in amazement. "It's so beautiful! I can't believe we are here!" She hopped down and ran over to Seth who was still in his own world. "Come see!" She grabbed his hand, and pulled him over to the top step, overlooking the property. "Isn't it incredible?" Seth couldn't believe his eyes and stood there with his mouth slightly open. "Come on, let's go!"

Sovannah took off down the steps, hopping like a little schoolgirl full of excitement as Seth just stood there and stared out in front of him. The steps went down, about twenty feet, at roughly a forty-five degree angle, until the last stone disappeared into the sand below. The sand stretched out at least a hundred feet to a small cottage on the sand. To the left, the waves gently licked the shore as the sun bounced off the water. *The beach house! But how could it be? How can I be here now?*

He began descending the steps one by one, slowly, as he stared without blinking. The small wooded porch on the beach house was worn and aged, but completely intact. Nothing was broken or falling apart. The windows no longer were jagged and broken, but smooth and whole. The door hung perfectly on the hinges. The handle was still glistening in the sun. *I don't understand.*

Boxes were piled in several stacks. He looked at the sand that led from the house down to the water, and stared off into the horizon down the coast, picturing his first night as he ran and ran away from this place. He looked to his left out on the pristine blue water, to the far distant place where the sky and water met, wondering where he swam to, before sinking below the surface. As he reached the bottom, he fixated on the beach house as he stepped out of his sandals onto the sand with his bare feet. He took a few steps and felt the grains fall between his toes as he wiggled them under the surface. He closed his eyes and took a deep breath, taking in the smells around him. He thought about that night when he first woke on the dark beach, tired, naked, cold, alone, and confused. The place looked so different now. It felt more... real. More... alive.

"Come on, what are you waiting for? This is amazing!" Sovannah hopped and skipped like a child along the edge of the water, letting the waves rush up to her one by one, and the cool breeze toss her hair all around, smiling and laughing in pure enjoyment.

Seth didn't move or say a word. He just watched her play in the water in disbelief. A million thoughts and questions crashed together in his head as he stood there in the sand. He closed his eyes and hoped more than anything to be free. *Maybe it's finally over... Maybe this is the end...* A cold breeze blew through his hair as he thought about waking up to that darkness again. *No more... I can't take it again...* He raised his head and repeated the words silently to himself as a tear fell down his cheek toward the sand below. *Please don't ever send me back there...* The sounds of the water and the wind and the trees faded away. *Please...*

CHAPTER SIXTEEN

GLORIOUS DREAMS

11:37 a.m.
Sept. 7th, 2002
Liberum Medical Center
Springfield, IL

By the time the neurologist arrived, the boy's family, along with Charlie, had been sitting with him for a few hours already. The room was mostly quiet, save for the medical machines chirping and beeping in a pattern that eventually faded into the background for each of them.

The young ones, Marcus and Mariah, were near the windows with Charlie, looking down at the cars driving by on the street. Gail and Arthur sat side by side in chairs near the foot of the bed. Gail rested her head on his shoulder, and occasionally used it to catch falling tears. Michelle and Brian stood near the head of the boy's bed, watching the machine pump air into his lungs and talking among themselves. On the other side of the bed were Ryan and Rachel. Every so often Ryan attempted to lighten the mood with a joke or a funny observation about a nurse or hospital worker. It rarely worked.

They were all losing their patience when finally the door opened and a nurse peaked her head in. "The neurologist has arrived. He will be in shortly to run some tests. He will need some room in here too, so I need to ask that all of you except the young man's parents leave the ward until he is finished. You can head back to the waiting area, or if you are interested, the lunch bar in the cafeteria on the first floor is open. The food is surprisingly good here too."

She said all this with a cheerful smile on her face, which failed to be contagious. Ryan smiled back, understanding how hard it must be for her to keep the pain of the families she meets out of her own life.

"Lunch sounds good to me. Who's in?" Ryan reached out for Rachel's hand and scanned the room for takers.

Charlie was the first to speak up. "I'm in. I haven't eaten in a long time."

"Yeah, let's leave Mom and Dad alone." Michelle took charge as usual. "Kids, let's go get something to eat." She reached down and put her hand on top of Gail's. "You and Dad gonna be okay here?"

Gail squeezed her hand back. "Yeah, thanks. Bring me back a water, ok?"

"Sure, you want anything, Dad?"

Arthur just shook his head no without saying a word. His stoicism meant to camouflage his fear.

"Well, if you think of anything you need, call my cell or text me and I'll bring it back. Don't worry, the tests will turn out fine, and the news will be good." She turned to the nurse in the doorway. "How long do we need to be gone?"

The nurse continued in her cheery tone. "Depending on what tests he has to run, it can be as short as an hour, or as long as three. I can't really say. But you can call the ward to find out if you want."

Michelle turned back to Gail. "Just get a hold of me when he's done, okay? I'll have my phone by my side. I want to be here to get the news with you. Don't worry, it will be all right. Soon we will find out when he will get to wake up, and when we get to talk to him again. Just stay positive."

Gail couldn't even speak at this point. She just nodded her head and waved goodbye.

"Come on, Brian. Kids, let's go."

The six of them, along with Charlie, headed out the door and stopped at the washing station to remove their gowns, before heading down to the cafeteria. Charlie fiddled with his phone in his pocket, but fought the urge to take it out.

About forty minutes passed before the nurse opened the door again and walked into the room. Behind her was another doctor, tall and thin, with deep eyes, spectacles, and a thick mustache. He was carrying a large case in one hand, and a metal clipboard holding several papers in the other hand. He set the items on the cart next to the patient's bed and reached out his hand to Arthur and Gail.

"I'm Dr. Cushing. Sorry it took me so long. I got held up on another patient."

Gail and Arthur shook his hand and attempted to smile back at him.

"I believe you have been told already why I'm here. I'm going to run some tests on your son's brain to determine his level of neural activity, and also some tests to examine the responsiveness of his sensory perceptions and functionality.

Hopefully the results will shed some light on his future, and what kind of obstacles he might be facing. When I'm done, I'll do my best to answer any questions you might have."

"Thank you." Gail and Arthur spoke in unison. They sat and watched as he opened the complicated looking case and took out several smaller instruments, along with a larger electronic device with many wire attachments. The doctor proceeded to unbutton the young man's robe and place small white discs all over his chest, arms, face, and head. These discs were taped in place and connected to the electronic device one by one using long wires. He plugged it in and a muffled whirring hung in the air as the components inside the device spun and came to life.

During the next hour and a half, beeps and zips and whirrs filled the air. The machine's electronic readouts were meaningless to Arthur and Gail, but with each view of the device, the doctor furiously wrote on his forms and filled out his graphs. Sensors were moved and repositioned continuously on the body, as he pressed and poked and touched him with countless instruments of various shapes, sizes, and materials. The torturous minutes seemed to drag on as Arthur and Gail sat, wondering what it all meant.

All the while, their son lay motionless and lifeless, providing no visible feedback to the doctor's probes. Gail's eyes were wide as she watched the doctor move from one side of the bed to the other, pressing buttons, moving wires, jotting down notes, and touching him. It was as if she expected at any moment her son might wake up. That she might be able to talk to him soon.

Finally, after two hours and forty eight minutes, the doctor began pulling the sensors off and packing the instruments away in his case. As he re-buttoned the young man's gown, he spoke without turning away from him.

"I have to head down to the lab and have the results processed. Unfortunately, depending on how busy the lab is, this can take a while. You can let the other family members know they can come back if they would like. I'll have the nurses inform you when I plan to return."

He finished the gown and clipped his pen back onto his clipboard. He closed the case and picked it up, turning back to Arthur and Gail, who seemed eager for immediate feedback.

"Is he going to be okay?" Gail spoke with hesitation and fear in her voice.

"Honestly, I can't know until I get the results from the tests. The data is all stored in this machine, and I have to get it to the lab and let the computers crunch the numbers. I've seen these things turn out every which way possible, and I don't like to hypothesize without the data. I'm sure you understand." He reached his hand out to Arthur. "But I'll come back here as soon as I have the results, I promise."

After shaking hands, he smiled at both of them and walked out the door. Gail immediately reached for her phone and sent Michelle a text message as promised.

#

Charlie and the rest of the family rushed back. As they walked in the door to his room, their eyes focused on the bed, each of them partly hoping that he would be sitting in the bed awake, chatting with Gail and Arthur upon their arrival. Even though they knew there was little chance, they were all still slightly disappointed to see that nothing had really changed since they left.

Charlie thought about his son Michael as he looked at the boy, and wondered if he had overstayed his welcome at this point.

"Maybe I should just take off. I don't want to intrude…"

Gail immediately quieted those thoughts. "Don't be silly, Charlie. I want you to say hello to him when he wakes up." Charlie smiled and resumed his position along the wall near the windows, still fighting the urge to take out his phone and listen to the message for the thousandth time.

Michelle gave Gail a hug and handed her the water bottle she requested. She tried her best to make small talk as Gail took a sip.

"Sorry if your water is a bit warm. That took a lot longer than we expected. We ended up just wandering around the hospital, and went outside for some fresh air. We found a cute little gift shop on the first floor, too. I'll take you there sometime when you need a break from this room."

Gail attempted a thankful smile. "How was the food?"

"It was okay. They have a nice salad bar you would like."

Brian and Ryan both agreed that the food was actually pretty good for hospital food.

Michelle's relentless optimism continued. "Keep your head up, Mom. Just think about what you will say to him when he wakes up. I promise it will be good news when the doctor returns."

"But…"

"No buts! Just stay positive. You don't need to keep doing that to yourself. You will drive yourself crazy. So just try to have good thoughts, ok? Keep the faith."

Gail looked at her sheepishly. "I'll try."

They all waited together for the next two hours, going in shifts to the restrooms, and taking periodic walks down the hall to the vending machines, just to think about something else for a while, or keep the children from getting too antsy.

The room remained silent for most of the two hours, except for the shuffle of pacing feet and impatient sighs. Brian passed some time querying Charlie for more details of the crash, which led to other stories about Charlie's life before his son Michael's accident. He told Brian about his Michael's passion for cars, and how Michael used to keep posters in his room of all the cars he hoped one day to drive. "He Loved Mustangs, my boy. I was always a Pontiac man, but for some reason, he wanted a Mustang. A silver one. He was fond of one model in particular; the Shelby GT 500. I bet he had five or six posters of just that one car. Even had a few models that he put together of it. Always painted them silver too. Never any other color."

Brian listened intently, offering only the occasional few words. "That's a nice one."

"I told him to save his money if he wanted one, because his old man could never afford one. But I swear, I'd sell everything I own to get him one now." Charlie fought back the tears during his stories, all the while clutching his phone in his pocket.

The stories between Charlie and Brian, and the crying from various parts of the room, and the pulsing of the machines continued, until the sun began to dip below the tree line outside the window. Everyone was reaching the limits of their patience when the door finally opened.

Dr. Cushing stepped in, holding a clipboard and a couple of folders. He flashed a slight manufactured smile on his face, but a look of concern seemed to easily show through. Everyone gathered near Gail and Arthur without being told, eager for good news.

Dr. Cushing lowered himself slightly onto the foot of the bed near the young man's feet. He held the clipboard in front of him with both hands.

"I hope your wait wasn't too unbearable. I tried to rush the results along the best I could, but the lab is quite backed up right now."

Everyone just stared at him, without responding. Their eyes were eager and locked in on his. Arthur put his hand on Gail's. Every second of silence felt like an eternity as they awaited the news. The doctor could sense their need for answers, and ceased with the small talk.

"I'd like to go over the results of the tests with you before I answer any big questions you might have."

Arthur nodded to him to continue and felt Gail's hand grip his even tighter.

"I performed an Electroencephalography test on your son. You might have heard of this referred to more commonly as an EEG. An EEG uses sensors attached to the patient's head to measure the level of electrical activity in the brain. This gives us a reading of the amount of alpha and beta waves present in the hemispheres."

He could see that the family cared little for any scientific talk, and simply wanted to know the results. He tried his best to cut to the chase.

"In this case, the EEG showed almost zero electrical current in the readouts. As you can probably ascertain, this is not good news."

Gail immediately started crying uncontrollably and buried her head in Arthur's shoulder.

"You said almost. Does that mean there is some activity going on inside his head?" Michelle was struggling to keep her optimism.

"An EEG can often pick up tiny amounts of electrical current present in the room, generated by the life support machines, or even everyday items such as cell phones, lights, etc... However, there is a minimum threshold to allow for this in the tests that the patient must exceed for us to consider the results positive. Your son's results were far below this level."

Ryan shifted his weight in his chair nervously. "But he's in a coma. Wouldn't the brain activity be low because of that?"

The doctor turned towards Ryan. "That's a fair question actually. And EEG is meant to just give us an idea of where his activity level is. There are certain functions that even in a coma continue, such as breathing and the contraction of the heart. In some cases of severe coma, the levels can be so low that more testing is necessary. In this case, after seeing the initial readout, I also did a follow up SSEP test. This type of test uses small instruments and diodes placed on the body to provide manual stimulus to the nerve endings, with an emphasis on the median nerve. Electrodes are then placed on the patient's head to measure the responsiveness in the brain of these stimuli on various parts of the body."

"What kind of stimulus are you talking about?"

"Localized pressure is applied first, and if this is unsuccessful it is followed by small electric shocks in specific areas. These shocks are harmless, but are strong enough to let us know that the brain has registered the electricity."

Gail squeezed Arthur's hand even harder. His shirt muffled her weeping, but everyone could still hear it. Her tears only seemed to make everyone else's eyes water even more than they already were.

"During this second test, his brain showed no response to the either the pressure tests or the electrical shocks."

Nearly everyone in the room had tears in their eyes by now, still trying to cling to hope that at the end of all this, the doctor would have good news.

"The results were fairly conclusive and this tells us that his brain is no longer capable of responding to messages sent by any part of his body."

Arthur finally broke his long streak of silence. His raspy voice was deep and powerful, and commanded attention. "What does it mean?"

The doctor looked into Arthur's eyes. "Essentially, it means that without the help of these machines, his lungs cannot breathe on their own and his heart cannot beat on its own. The body has basically stopped working, and aside from a few inconsequential blips and spikes, the brain has stopped working too. There is no sign of consciousness."

Gail raised her head and looked at the doctor through her tears. "I know there is life in my boy. I can feel it."

The doctor took a deep breath. It was always difficult to relay messages such as these. "I'm very sorry. His body shows no medical signs of sustainable life. He is not capable of cognitive thinking, and we feel there is likely no chance of him ever recovering from his present condition."

"No chance? How can you say that?"

"I do not wish to crush your spirits, but I also do not wish to give you false hope. That can often times be more emotional and devastating for a family. Therefore, I try to just give the facts as best as I can. I can say that even today, science only knows a finite amount about the human body and the uncertainties of life and death. And we know even less about the complex inner workings of the human mind. Although little can be said with absolute certainty, we must go by our wealth of previous experience and probabilities. I am saddened and sympathetic for you, but also confident in what the results tell me."

Michelle, finally out of optimism, stepped over to the bed and knelt down beside it. Her tears poured onto his hospital gown and she squeezed his hand as she began weeping uncontrollably. "Please wake up, brother! Wake up! God please let him wake up…" Brian rushed over and held onto her, rubbing her back as she cried.

Gail stood up and walked over to the doctor. Arthur followed suit and put his arm around her as she stopped. She struggled to speak, but needed frankness. "Is my boy going to die?" Her lips were shaking so much that the words could just barely be understood. Her eyes were deep and darkened from all the crying.

The doctor stood up as she stepped over to him. "To answer your question the best I can, I must say that all of my medical knowledge and experience says that…"

Even the doctor struggled to complete the sentence as he saw the pain that Gail was going through. He took a deep breath.

"…that your son is *already* dead."

The words seemed to shake everyone at their core. The air seemed to leave the room as the doctor continued.

"Technically, his body is hanging on with the assistance of machines, but clinically, the brain is under the threshold that we can call living."

Gail reached out and placed her hand on his leg. In a rare moment of strength, she spoke clearly. "I can feel him. He is still here with us. His soul is still strong. It still has life. I know he's in there somewhere, hanging on. I just know…"

The doctor often heard these sorts of things from family members and never knew what to say to them. Hope is a powerful thing that knows no limits. Nothing he could say could possibly compete with or deny the hope that they felt, but he issued his standard response, perhaps with more emotion this time than any time before.

"I'm sorry, Mrs. Ashling but we have done everything we can to help him. There is nothing more we can do at this point for his body. Some things simply cannot be fixed. I am very sorry."

Hearing those words, the boy's brother, Ryan, became overwhelmed for the first time by his emotions and he darted out of the room. The door slammed behind him. Rachel quickly stood and rushed after him. The others could hear his sobbing in the main part of the ward, interrupted by the occasional anger filled "Why!!" or "No!!"

Gail stood there in shock. Her hands shook uncontrollably. After several moments, she spoke through falling tears and a cracking voice. "I can't let him go yet. I'm not ready." The doctor saw the pain in her eyes as she turned and looked at Arthur. "And he is not ready. He hasn't finished school... or bought a house... or been in Love. It can't be over. Tell me there is something we can do for our boy." Her words were filled with fear, but no one had answers for her. Arthur just held her as she buried her face in his chest. No one spoke for several seconds, as the sounds of beeping machines made their presence known again.

The silence was broken by Arthur's deep voice penetrating the air. "Doc... what comes now? What do we do?"

The doctor wiped his lips and then ran his thumb along his brow, as he had nervously done a hundred times when he had to give bad news. The door opened slowly and Ryan and Rachel walked back into the room and stood in the back. The doctor's words had a sorry tone to them and came out slowly, as if to ease the weight they carried.

"I'm afraid that your only decision left to make now is how long to keep him on life support. These machines can keep his heart pumping and his lungs breathing for now. But I need to be honest with you. Since this is optional for the family, most insurance companies do not cover life support once it is determined that the patient cannot be revived. If you pay for it out of your own pockets it can be outrageously expensive. It can cripple a family. I've seen families empty their savings accounts, wipe out their retirements, and sell their homes trying to keep a Loved one alive on machines for as long as they can. But my experience tells me it is never worth it."

He paused for a second to rub his other brow with his thumb.

"I know it's a lot to think about. I just want you to have all the information for when you make the decision. And I don't want you to sacrifice your family's future… simply clinging to hope that he will have one. I don't see any chance at all that he will ever regain consciousness."

Arthur rubbed the back of Gail's head and looked into the doctor's eyes. "I know you're just trying to help." He took a deep breath and exhaled slowly. "When do we have to decide?"

"My report has already been submitted to Dr. Kaplan. He will review it in the morning and then will come talk to you about your wishes. Take the rest of tonight to talk it over amongst yourselves." Arthur nodded in acknowledgement as the doctor continued. "I also need to ask that you discuss the option of donating his organs. He is young, and his body is in good shape. I know this day has been filled with bad news, and this is the last thing you want to think about, but you need to consider the idea that he could save the lives of several people once his has completed." The doctor stood up and reached his hand out to Arthur. "I'm sorry I didn't have better news for you all, but please think these things over."

Arthur and Brian each shook the doctor's hand before he left the room. As the door shut behind him they were all left in silence again. No one was willing to speak first.

Charlie thought about his son Michael and what he

went through that night he passed away. He knew the sinking feeling that each of the boy's family members had in their hearts. He felt sorry for them in a way that only he could. Yet despite what the doctor said, part of him was still clinging to hope that a miracle would wake him up and let him walk out the front door of the hospital with his family.

An hour passed filled with crying and taking turns stepping up to the bed. Michelle looked Arthur in the eyes as Gail buried her face and wept again.

"I can't believe we have to talk about this." The last few words of the sentence trailed off and blended seamlessly into sniffles and tears. She turned to Brian. "How do they expect us to make these decisions tonight? I can't even think about it."

He didn't know what else to say so he simply shrugged his shoulders. No one knew what to say. They all simply exchanged glances and looks of bewilderment, eyes red and puffy from tears. Marcus and Mariah didn't fully understand what was going on, but cried along with everyone else in the room.

The next couple of hours were filled with lots of pacing, crying, and tear-filled discussions about how they could financially afford to keep him alive, and about his wishes in regards to organ donation.

"There's no way he would want…"

"How could you possibly know that, have you ever talk to…"

"I'm telling you, he…"

During the more heated parts of the conversation, Charlie shrunk into the corner trying to keep to himself, and trying to keep the children occupied by talking to them about their school or other lighthearted things, to distract them from the adults. Gail seemingly tried to absorb herself into Arthur's shoulder, and then into the blanket after he stood to stretch his legs.

The sun was completely gone by now, and everyone was emotionally and physically exhausted from the events of the day and the conversations at hand. At some point they knew they had to sleep, and maybe even eat something if they could, and no sense of agreement could be found between everyone in the room.

"I'm just saying that there's no way…" Michelle trailed off mid-sentence. They had been so completely engulfed in the conversation that no one else in the room had noticed Gail finally gathering herself and was standing up. But as soon as they saw her, the talk quickly died down into silence, as they could tell she had something to say to them all. Her eyes were so tired of crying she looked almost sick. Her voice was broken and raspy. Yet her tone commanded their attention. "It's late. You haven't eaten in hours. Why don't all of you just go get something to eat, then head back to the hotel and get some rest? You can come back here in the morning."

"What do you mean? Without you?" Michelle looked at her with a puzzled look on her face.

"I'm going to stay here alone with him tonight." She squeezed his toes through his hospital booties.

Ryan stepped a little closer to her. "We're not just going to leave you here all alone."

"I'll be fine. You can go. I'll have some food sent to the room." She knew she wouldn't be able to eat, but she said it anyway.

Michelle said what everyone was thinking. "What are we going to tell the doctors tomorrow?"

Gail looked at the floor for a second, then into her eyes. "I don't know." She looked over at her son, lying there motionless. She was hoping he would just sit up and end all of this. He would know what to do. He always did. If she could just ask him…

"But I'll figure it out. Just let me be alone with him tonight."

Michelle couldn't stand the thought of her crying alone all night. "I'll stay with you then."

"I want to be alone." Gail's voice seemed much stronger this time.

"You shouldn't…"

"Stop!" Arthur's tone trumped the others. His authority was still strong as the leader of the family when it needed to be. Michelle immediately got quiet.

"Your mom already told you. She knows what she wants. And she can handle herself. If she wants to stay alone, she can. That's the end of it. So let's head out." He kissed Gail on the cheek and whispered something into her ear. She assured him she would be okay, and he stepped towards the door. The rest of group knew the argument was over. They took turns hugging her on the way out until she was the last person in the room. She stood in front of her boy's bed, squeezing his foot under the blanket. The room seemed silent again until the humming of the machines and the incessant beeping crept back into the void left.

She pulled up a chair next to the bed and sat beside him, rubbing his arm. She stared at his face and imagined him smiling. Her memory of his smile was so strong that she could almost see him doing it now. He seemed so peaceful lying there, and as she watched his chest rise and fall in tune with the gasping of the machines, she pretended he was simply napping, having the most glorious dreams.

CHAPTER SEVENTEEN

INTO THE DARKNESS

Minutes seemed to pass in the time it took the tear to leave Seth's eye and land on the sand at his feet. Behind closed eyes, he pictured Sovannah running across the beach like a little girl. His thoughts still raced in his head. He looked back on each moment with her, from the time they met to now. Had years felt to him like moments? Or had moments felt to him like years? *Were these dreams of my future... Or were they memories of my past...*

He was tired. Tired of thinking. Tired of crying. Tired of wondering what's real and what's not. He finished his prayer for this all to be over. For him to open his eyes and see Sovannah running up to him to welcome him to their new home. For the colors of this world to never fade back into that darkness. *That cold.*

He was afraid to open his eyes. For the first time he had hope that this was all over. *I can't go through it all again. I can't lose her anymore.*

He wiggled his toes and still felt the sand slide between them. He peeled open one eye, then the other, slowly, like a child peeking out from under the protective covers in bed. He stared straight ahead of him, as his expression faded to nothing. He couldn't move. He was frozen in the moment by an emotion he couldn't describe. His stomach sank inside him. His skin seemed to tighten around his bones. His knees buckled and crashed to the sand at his feet.

His prayer went unanswered.

He was kneeling in the exact same spot as he had stood and watched Sovannah running towards the water. His cheek still had a trail from the tear that fell only moments ago. It was glistening in the moonlight. Yet, Sovannah was gone. It all was gone. The breeze... the warmth... the color... all vanished... along with his hope. For one brief moment he felt as if this all had come to an end. And in the blink of an eye, it was taken from him again.

He peeked behind him and saw nothing. The stones and stairs that he just walked were gone, along with the courtyard and trees above. A fog erased everything and seemed to sit just a few feet from where he now knelt. The weight of the air above him seemed to weigh him down. He felt crushed by the darkness around him.

Yet, no tears came. No sadness overwhelmed him. Instead he looked down and felt his blood slowly begin to boil. He sat there staring at the sand with his head lowered as his breaths came faster and faster. He wanted to call out for Sovannah but knew it was useless. He had tried that before. He knew she was gone now. A memory. A dream. He wasn't sure which. His veins flexed and pulsated in his neck. His skin turned red and his eyes filled with fire, bringing the only color to this lifeless place.

He had felt anger before, but not like this. This was more. This was the anger and rage of a tortured and beaten animal, cornered and trapped, ready to lash out at anything.

His lips clinched together and he stood slowly. He no longer felt like himself. He raised his eyes slowly and looked up at the moon hanging in the darkness. It seemed to smile back at him, mocking him, victorious once again.

Seth's rage could no longer be contained. He screamed at the moon in a violent filled eruption. "WHY?!?... WHY?!?... WHYYY?!" He picked up whatever sticks and rocks he could find in the sand and threw them at the moon, screaming the whole time. They simply crashed back to the sand some distance away from him, reabsorbed back into this place, as he had been.

"What do you want?! Why are you doing this to me?!"
Silence.
"Answer me!"
Yet no answer came. His eyes were dripping with anger filled tears as he shouted all around him.

"Who is doing this to me? God? What have I done? I don't deserve this!"
He looked around him for answers. "God? Is it you? Why won't you answer me? What is this place?"

He spun in circles in the sand, looking into the darkness in every direction. "Why bring me Sovannah just to take her away again?"

He turned toward the beach house and his eyes fell upon the tattered façade in front of him. Once again he could see the faint outline of the numbers that once hung on the house. He stared at them through his tears. *9064*. Rays of moonlight could be seen striking the broken glass of the window. He despised this place of torture.

His breath came faster and faster. His eyes were still red with anger. He ran up to the wooden deck and began throwing rocks and pieces of wood at the house. Shards of glass that barely hung in the window frame crashed to the wood below. He screamed and cried as he hurled everything he could, until he could find no more to throw. His blood still boiled.

"Why can't I have her? WHY?"

He ran up the steps and kicked the falling apart porch as hard as he could, breaking off a large section of wood. He grasped this wood like a sword and swung it at the railing, crashing it over and over as wood chunks flung into the air. He beat on the sides of the house and the window frames, shattering every last bit of the remaining glass. His hands clenched the wood with so much force that it began to cut his hands. Blood dripped to the wooden deck as he continued to swing, determined to knock this place to the ground, as tears dripped from his face.

The broken wood and tiny bits of glass beneath him dug into his feet. He kicked the door with all his might, and as his foot slammed back into the broken deck, a larger shard of the fallen glass deeply pierced the bottom of his foot. He let out a piercing scream as he let go of the wooden board and fell with a crash onto the bits of broken wood and glass. Blood poured from his feet, as he crawled on all fours to the sand, where he lay, defeated once again.

The pain throbbed all over his body, but inside he was even worse. He felt as if his heart was crushed, and his lungs were caved in from the weight of this place. He was beaten down to his lowest point, and his rage was replaced by hopelessness. His expression slowly changed from anger to a blank and shallow stare, as he looked out onto the dark waters.

He remembered how he nearly drowned out there, sinking deeper, watching the moonlight fade to darkness above him. *I wish I would have just died that day...*

He closed his eyes and gathered the strength to stand, ignoring the pain and blood that left him. He wiped the tears from his eyes, smearing blood and sand across his face. He looked back at the beach house behind him.

No more...

He turned away and took a few steps down the beach, into the darkness, into the nothingness. This time he spoke aloud. "Never again... You hear me? Are you listening now? I'm done. I'm done with your stupid game. " He vowed to never again enter the beach house. No more clues. No more experiences. No more glimpses of Sovannah. No more leaving her.

"No more pain."

He walked in a line directly away from the beach house, along the edge of the water. There was nothing in front of him, and no hope that there ever would be, but he didn't care.

"I'd rather die than be taken from her again."

He kept walking. Without looking back. Into the fog. Into the darkness. Into the unknown.

CHAPTER EIGHTEEN

AN OLD SOUL

7:37 a.m.
Sept. 8th, 2002
Liberum Medical Center
Springfield, IL

The morning light streaked through the blinds at a shallow angle. Strips of light stretched across the room slowly, as the sun rose in the morning sky. Warmth began to fill the room. As the light reached the hospital bed it crawled across the blankets and up to the boy's face. He lay motionless, unaware of the rays falling softly across his face, warming his skin.

Gail's head was resting on the back of the chair next to the hospital bed. When the light reached her eyelids, she peeled them back and watched the rays glisten and bounce off his skin. She had stayed up most of the night by his side, watching the machines assist his breathing, and thinking about the looming questions her family would have, until the noises in the room faded away, and she was finally able to sleep for a few hours.

She stretched her neck, tight from sleeping in a chair, and tense from the emotions of the last twenty-four hours. Seeing the sunlight on his face brought a smile to hers, as she remembered how much he Loved being in the sun growing up. She sat for a while looking out the window at the sun and holding his hand, trying to put off the impossible for as long as she could. She was given a task no mother would ever want. She was to decide the fate of her own child. The slow and gentle rise and fall of his chest comforted her, and reminded her of when he was just a baby. Even then, she would hold him in her arms and watch his tiny chest rise and fall, afraid that it might stop. She couldn't bear the thought of either of her two options, as both were equally horrible to her. Letting him go to slip into the vast unknown of death was an unthinkable thought. Yet forcing him to live like this… by machine… unable to breath or beat his own heart… for possibly years… was also unthinkable. *How can I make this decision? If only he would just wake up…*

That would solve everything, she thought. He would wake and walk out of the room with her, hand in hand, and head outside where he could feel the sunlight on his face for real. And when the rest of the family showed up, there would be only tears of joy. No decisions would have to be made, except possibly what to do with the rest of the day.

She clung to this hope and prayed, rummaging through her memories of him. She thought about how he used to stand outside in the yard, facing the sunlight, and close his eyes and raise his head, arms stretched wide on either side of him, taking it all in, letting the light warm his face. He seemed almost lost in those moments, as if time stood still for him.

    She remembered how sometimes she would look out the window at their old house and watch him playing outside with his younger brother and his friends. He was always different from the other boys. He seemed to be fascinated by things the other kids ignored, and sometimes when he was alone, he would spend hours outside, just experiencing and inspecting the complexities of nature. He had a thirst to learn that was unquenchable, and as a young man, he had hung on to this childlike awe of the world. Gail Loved this about him, and was proud that he had stayed this way. Her pride came through when she spoke of him to her friends and family, and they could see her eyes beaming with every word.

    She held his hand and gently rubbed his head. By now the sun had filled the room and Gail noticed a glare shining off of an object in the corner of the room. She walked over to its origin and pulled the box of his belongings from under the chair where Charlie had left them. The sun was gleaming off a metal bookmark. She picked up the box and took it over to her chair next to his bed and began looking through it for the first time since Charlie gave it to her. Tears formed in her eyes as she picked up each item. Books he had held in his hands in the days leading up to the accident... Pens he had written his thoughts and dreams with... CDs that he had listened to while walking to class or driving to a movie with his friends... The family saw him less and less after he left for college, and she missed him, but she was proud of the changes she saw in him, the young man that he had become, and the life that she knew he would achieve. These items were all pieces of that life, and pieces of him. Her tears continued to fall as she thought about the role each item played in his life.

At the bottom of the box, she noticed something pink and reached through the pile of stuff to get it. It was soft to the touch. She pulled it out of the box and held it up in front of her. It was a small pink cardigan, dirty and torn on the side. Three little ivory buttons adorned the neck, and a tiny ring of tattered lace around the waistline. It obviously belonged to a girl, and from what Gail could tell, a petite girl at that. She rubbed the fabric with her fingers, and a puzzled look appeared on her face. *What is this doing in here? Whose is it?*

She folded the cardigan neatly and placed it back in the box, next to the beat up journal. She stared at the cover, knowing that it was filled with his personal thoughts and dreams. She hesitated before pulling it out of the box, partially because she thought it might be private, and partially because she knew it would make her cry. As she flipped through it, she stopped here and there to read a quote or a small excerpt from one of his poems. She read his words slowly, taking them in, often stopping to wipe the tears from her eyes. She had never read his poetry before, and as she perused the words, she felt she could almost hear his voice, reciting the words out loud to her…

…Wake me up and ask me why
I stare into the sunlit sky
Or dream of soaring on the high
Forever in the by and by…

…Be this night the night of dreams
And all that passed before
Fall into forgotten seams
On far forsaken shores…

…Meet me in the secrets of the mind

And run with me to places still unknown
Lose yourself in all that we may find
To be with me together and alone...

She was always amazed at how her son always seemed to think like an adult, even at a young age. She used to call him an old soul. Sometimes it was like he was looking back on his life from a distance, with the regrets and thoughts of an old man, even in the present.

...And joyful it is to be free
Where none can follow my way
And often a lifetime is spent
In the single escape of a day...

Page after page she turned, as pieces of his heart and soul stretched out to her through his words. She wondered if he could somehow help her with her decision. What would he want her to do? *Talk to me son...*

...Though longed for in the eager hearts of men
And searched for in the distant skies above
Eternity is not the journey's end
But found in every second spent in Love...

...And maybe I have walked these very shores before
But never as it now had seemed
And maybe life and death are simply doors
Among the many hallways I have dreamed...

She had been reading for nearly an hour when she came upon a page with a dog-eared corner near the end of the journal. It was a longer poem, but the title caused her to stop and read the whole thing. By the look on her face, the words seemed to touch her even more than anything she had read to this point. She finished and read it again. As she read the final line again, a few of her tears overstayed their welcome in her eyes, and fell onto the pages below, smearing the ink a little in one spot. She read it in its entirety at least three times before looking over at him. She squeezed his hand, and rubbed his arm.

The sunlight streaked through the window and she stood up to face it, letting the light shine on her face. She closed her eyes and raised her arms, just as he used to, spreading them wide with her palms faced up. She stood there in the warmth, taking it all in, lost in thoughts and memories. A slight smile appeared on her face and a moment of peace seemed to greet her.

When she opened her eyes, she kissed him on the forehead and whispered in his ear.

"I Love you, buddy."

She sat and laid her head against the back of the chair, resting her eyes and mind. Forty minutes were spent motionless and silent, in deeper rest than she had had all night, until the sound of the door opening woke her.

Dr. Cushing stepped into the room.

"I hope your night wasn't too terrible."

Gail attempted a smile, and nodded slightly, choosing to remain silent. The doctor took that hint to mean she didn't really want to elaborate.

"I thought I'd let you know that the rest of your family has arrived. I told them I would step in here and let you know you before I let them in."

"It's okay. You can let them in." Gail stretched her neck again and rubbed her eyes.

The doctor opened the door and waived them all in.

They filed in one by one, each looking like they had the same kind of night that she had. Charlie gravitated towards the corner of the room again by the window, and the rest took turns giving hugs to Gail as the doctor shut the door behind them.

"I'm going to let you all have some time to chat alone in here. It's approaching nine-thirty now. I'll be back here around ten and we can go over your options and fill out any life support or donor paperwork if necessary. If you have any questions in the meantime, you can tell one of the nurses to page me, and I'll come right away."

Michelle nodded in agreement and he turned and walked out of the room. Before the door even shut everyone in the room had their eyes fixed on Gail.

Arthur put his arm around her. "Were you alright last night?"

"I survived. Mostly I just prayed that he would wake up and talk to me. I miss my boy."

"Me too, honey… me too." He squeezed her as he said the words.

Gail looked at Michelle. "What did you guys have for dinner last night?"

Michelle hesitated before answering. "We just found a place."

The look on her face told Gail she didn't care to discuss dinner so she turned to Brian. "Did you guys sleep okay last night?" Brian simply nodded. She looked at Ryan and he gave only a nod as well. She could tell that no one was really interested in small talk this morning. They all just stared at her, and wanted to know the same thing. What had she decided? What are they going to do about everything? She stepped over to the hospital bed and ran her fingers through her son's hair. Everyone gathered around his bed. She looked at each of them, one by one, and could see in their eyes various versions and amounts of fear, anxiety, sadness, and empathy. Nearly all of them had tears in their eyes.

A few seconds passed and then she began. "I…"

She only made it through one word on her first try, and looked down at him again. She squeezed his hand and her eyes filled with tears.

Arthur placed his hand on top hers.

"It's okay. Whatever you have to say, we support it. We Love him and we Love you."

She wiped her eyes and looked at them all again.

"I… I've decided…" She took a deep breath, and a tear fell from her eye. It seemed to fall in slow motion towards the hospital bed as they all waited for what was to follow.

"…to let Seth go…"

CHAPTER NINETEEN

THE BLINDING FLOOD

The darkness seemed to stretch on for eternity in front of Seth. Each step was filled with determination, and he pressed his heels into the sand with greater and greater force. His eyes were fixed in front of him, focused on his objective, and unwavering in his dissent. The moon was bright above him and at an angle that cast but a tiny shadow directly beneath him. His breath, which was powerful and quick earlier, had slowed to a constant rhythm and could be seen in the air in front of him.

The final tears had fallen from his eyes onto the sand below awhile back, and the last of the curses had left his mouth. He let go of his anger and gave in to the hopelessness. He no longer questioned his situation, or pled for answers to the mysteries of this place or its meaning. He simply walked, with no agenda or purpose, towards nothing, and away from everything.

He tried not to think, but his thoughts always went back to Sovannah. The images of her couldn't be kept from his mind. *The way she looked so innocent sitting under the tree reading her book the day they first met... The moment he fell in Love as they looked at the stars above.* He looked up at the stars above him now and wondered if maybe she was somewhere doing the same thing. *The smell of her hair as she cuddled with him in front of the fireplace... The smoothness of her skin as it brushed against his in the hot tub on the ship...*

Yet, he wondered even more about the memories that he didn't have. *The proposal... The wedding... The years that disappeared in between...* He had no recollection of these moments, and wondered if they even existed at all. *Maybe none of it was real... Maybe Sovannah was just a dream all along... Maybe this is the dream...* He looked down at his hand and saw that he was still wearing a ring. He stopped walking and pulled it from his finger, staring at the smooth metal shining in the moonlight from above. *None of it's real... It's all meaningless... It's all an illusion... It's an illusion I don't want any part of anymore...* He stood there silent and stoic, staring out upon the waters before him, and closed his eyes. With all his strength he flung the ring as far as he could out into the dark waters. *Goodbye, Sovannah...*

As the ring hit the water somewhere out on the horizon, a slight breeze blew the hairs hanging over his forehead. He opened his eyes and peered into the darkness in front of him. In that moment he felt a change in the air and strained to see as far as he could out into the distance. His hair blew again. Something was different in the thickness surrounding him. He turned his head left and right, looking down the beach in both directions, but could see nothing. Emptiness was all around him, but something told him there was a difference. He took a deep breath and let it out, watching it form a haze in the cold air that surrounded him.

He turned back to face the water and stared into the distance as the breeze blew his hair once more. He squinted, shading his brow with his hand, as he peered into the vast emptiness in front of him. Suddenly, somewhere way out among the fog, he noticed the tiniest of lights on the distant water. His eyes widened as the light began to grow. He looked closely, wondering what could be the origin. *A star? A ship?*

Time seemed to stop in that one moment as his eyes and brain struggled to understand what they were seeing, and then, in an instant, he was blinded by a flood of light so bright that he had to shield his eyes and turn away for a second. He knew immediately what he was seeing. *The sun!*

The bright light burst through the fog with an intensity that seemed to part the seas before him in an attempt to reach out to him. The endless abyss of darkness was pierced all around him and the sun was like an immense train emerging from a dark tunnel in an instant, blasting its powerful light out at him with infinite force and strength. He shielded his eyes as the sun rose slowly and deliberately, like a conquering emperor, riding triumphantly into a new land.

As the sun rose even higher, Seth saw the blanket haze of fog that sat menacingly upon the water gradually disappear before his eyes. As it faded out of sight, he saw for the first time the distant waters that reached as far as his eyes could see to meet the horizon. He stared out upon the wonder before him, paralyzed by the power of the sun, and marveling at its ability to cut through the darkness of this place. It was a darkness so powerful and heavy that Seth felt until this moment it could not be overcome by anyone or anything, yet he watched as the distant waters were slowly brought to life.

As the sun climbed higher in the sky, it overpowered the moon above him more and more with each second that ticked by. He looked up at the moon, reluctant to share the same sky with this new sun, and struggling to hang on to its post in a losing battle. He smiled, as it began to fade away, and laughed as a deep blue invaded the blackness above him and all around him.

The sun gently began to turn an almost magical shade of yellow, and off in the distance, on the horizon just below it, Seth could see the dark oil-like waters start to turn a bright shade of turquoise. These were the most brilliant colors Seth had seen in this place, and he could hear off in the distance the sound of waves crashing into each other. He listened as the sounds grew louder and louder, and he could feel it all rushing towards him, eager to overwhelm him. The sounds… the colors… the light…

He raised his head to the sun and closed his eyes, feeling the rays push away the cold air that gripped him. He felt warmth on his face for the first time in this place, and smiled as the backs of his eyelids glowed like two tiny red blankets covering his eyes. He raised his arms and spread them wide, holding this pose for several seconds as he felt the light embrace his body and pierce his soul, filling him with peace and anticipation, as the sounds grew louder, and the light grew brighter still.

CHAPTER TWENTY

SUNLIGHT PARTED

10:00 a.m.
Sept. 8th, 2002
Liberum Medical Center
Springfield, IL

The words seemed to hang in the air after they left Gail's mouth. She could almost see them floating in the center of the room in front of everyone. Their eyes were fixed on her, as the words sank in to each of them. Truth be told, she wasn't entirely sure what she was going to say until she heard her own voice. Upon hearing it out loud, she seemed to finally be comfortable with her decision. *I've decided to let Seth go...*

Brian and Ryan both slowly lowered their eyes to the floor in unison, and Charlie seemed to sink even further into the corner. Michelle's lower lip began to stick out, and her eyes began to squeeze tight. The young ones didn't know exactly what was meant by the words, but they could tell it wasn't the news everyone was expecting.

Arthur put his arm around Gail tightly and they looked into each other's eyes. He spoke with weakness in his voice for the first time. "Is this what you really want?"

Gail's lips trembled as she saw the pain in his eyes. "Of course not. I want him to wake up. I want him to go home with us tonight. I want to talk to my boy again."

She reached over and squeezed Seth's hand. "But if that's not going to happen, then I think this is the only choice we can make."

"But..." Ryan lifted his head and managed only a single word out before his eyes filled with tears and his throat closed up.

Michelle spoke up and tried to finish his sentence. "How can we just... let him die?"

By now everyone was crying and had gathered close around Seth's bed. Gail ran her fingers through his hair and took a deep breath. "Because I think that's what he would want."

Michelle rubbed Seth's feet through his hospital booties. "Why would you think that?"

Gail looked over at the box of Seth's belongings in the chair. "His own words told me." She walked over to the box and pulled out the journal. She brought it back to the bed and turned to the poem near the back of the book with the dog-eared corner. "I want to read something to all of you."

They all stared at her with blank looks of anticipation on their faces. No one made a sound, and even the machines in the room seemed to quiet down to let her speak. She wiped the tears from her eyes and raised the book slightly. Her voice cracked at times, but as they heard the words, they thought about Seth, and pictured his voice reading aloud to each of them.

Sunlight Parted

When time has come to steal away the day
And barter me in laughter with the night
'Tis but for Love that I would choose to stay
If not, then let me seek the brilliant light

If I must live, then let me live in chase
Of that perfection I have dared in dreams
For what is life if filled with empty space
And what is sunlight parted from its beams

I shall not want if wanting cannot cease
I shall not stay if staying has but night
'Tis not a dream if waking brings decrease
'Tis not the day if daytime brings no light

So I must choose between two worlds apart
To wake and face what waking brings to view
Or stay asleep and nevermore depart
The place where I have dared to dream of you

September 5th 2002

    When she finished the last word, Gail simply stared at the page, knowing once again that she had made the right decision. "He wrote it the night before his accident."
    The blank stares on everyone's faces seemed to change at once to understanding. His words flew around in their

heads, calming their nerves, easing their minds. They accepted Gail's decision, and knew it was the right thing to do. They had to let Seth go, just like she said. They couldn't keep him trapped inside a dead body. One by one they all agreed.

"You're right mom." Michelle said while wrapping her arms around her mother's neck. "He wouldn't want to just lay here, trapped. He would want to be free."

Ryan spoke in a crackling voice. "How much time do we have?"

Gail could see the heartbreak in his eyes. "I'm not sure." She hugged him quickly and then stepped towards the door, turning to them once again before opening it. "I think Seth would want to help people the best he could. He Loved life too much. If he can save others in his death, then I'm going to let him. Another mother out there might get to talk to her boy again because of him. And knowing that makes this easier. I'm going to talk to the doctor now. I want you all to say goodbye to Seth."

As the door shut behind her, Arthur stepped up to Seth and the rest of the family seemed to fade away slightly, giving him time with his son. The rest followed in turn, one by one, saying goodbye and crying, squeezing Seth's hand, and hoping one last time that he might wake up. Ryan recalled stories of their youth, and told Seth how he always looked up to him. Michelle, Mariah, and Marcus could only cry, as Brian held them close by his side while they looked at Seth one last time.

Arthur looked at Charlie in the corner, and motioned him over to the side of Seth's bed. "I want you to know that we appreciate what you did for our boy, and for us." Charlie just nodded politely, and looked down at Seth, realizing he was the last person to see Seth awake. He was sad for his family, but thankful that they were all given the chance to say goodbye and be with him these last few hours. As he looked down at

Seth he felt a sense of relief come over him. He could feel the months of pain and regret leaving him as the words left his mouth.

"Seth, I know you don't know me at all, and I don't know you, but without knowing it, you've sort of given me a second chance at something, and for that I thank you. I'm sorry I wasn't able to get to you sooner, and I'm sorry I'll never get to meet you. For now all I can say is goodbye, and if you can hear me, maybe I can ask you for one small favor. If you bump into my boy Michael, please tell him I said I'm sorry and that I Love him." Charlie patted Seth on the shoulder and turned away, stopping momentarily to look back. "Oh, and tell him one more thing… tell him I said 'see ya when I see ya.'"

As he retreated back to the corner again, Charlie had a slight smile on his face. He seemed at peace finally. He closed his eyes and felt the exhaustion of the last several hours creeping in on him, and he pulled his phone from his pocket. He pressed a few buttons and held it to his year. After a few seconds he pulled the phone away from his face and looked down at the screen. He touched the word "Delete" with his finger, as the door opened again.

Gail and the doctor walked in, along with a nurse holding a clipboard. They all stepped up to Seth's bed and the doctor asked one final time about the family's wishes. Gail looked around the room and could tell from the faces that they all accepted her decision. She nodded and signed the papers, along with Arthur. Once this was done, they all stepped away to watch the doctors begin unhooking many of the machines keeping Seth alive.

When they completed, the doctor turned to face the entire group. "It shouldn't be long now. I'm very sorry for your loss. We will step outside now to give you some privacy in his final moments."

Every eye in the room was filled with tears, except those of Gail. She knew that very soon Seth would be freed, and in a better place, and this made her calm as she listened to the beeps get farther and farther apart.

Beep… beep…… beep……… beep…………… beep……………………………….

CHAPTER TWENTY-ONE

THE SONGS OF ANGELS

    The sun washed over Seth as he stood in the beams with his eyes closed and his arms spread wide, just as he did the day he first met Sovannah in college. The rays penetrated him and seemed to pass through his body, which was no match for the power before him. Serenity filled his entire existence, and for the first time, he was unafraid to re-open his eyes. He had no fear of what might be waiting for him.
    Slowly and calmly he lifted his eyelids and stared into the blinding light of the sun. It was a beauty like none he had ever seen anywhere in the world. Anywhere except in Sovannah's eyes. He smiled when he thought of her, and he stood there in total awe of the perfection before him. The water slowly crashed on the sand in front of him and streamed up to touch his toes. It was cool and light, refreshing to the

touch, and left his toes wet as it rushed back to the join the ocean. All around him the world teemed with beauty and life. Birds hovered in the distance just above the water. Bubbles popped in the sand as the water swept over it.

    He looked down at his body, and noticed the leather sandals on his feet, still wet from the tide. He pushed his toes into the sand and wiggled them in the soupy grains. His khaki shorts were warm in the sun, and his shirt blew in the wind, unbuttoned halfway and allowing the warm breeze to tickle the hairs on his body and his head. In the air he could smell the wonderful scents of the sea. The salt from the water seemed to stick to the insides of his nostrils, and the odor of fish and plants filled the air.

    He turned around and stared at the footprints in the sand, leading right up to where he now stood. They stretched out away from him, running off in the other direction towards the beach house steps, as if he had just ventured out for a morning stroll to catch the sunrise.

    To his left, he watched the trees that he never knew were here blowing in the breeze, along with the tall grasses that marked the border of the beach. He closed his eyes and listened to the wonderful sounds of the leaves and grass swaying in the wind, mixing with the sounds of the water and the birds. To Seth, it sounded like the songs of angels singing to him in a language only he could understand. As if it were a Love song written especially for him. He opened his eyes and the whole scene was filled with the most beautiful colors Seth had ever seen.

    His eyes eventually landed on the beach house. The once dark and desolate building that haunted him for so long resembled nothing of its former self. It was new and clean and perfect. Nothing was broken or missing. It was stripped of its power over him, and given instead a wonderful new aura, that captivated him and made him feel at peace. Now it only appeared to him as the most perfectly built and perfectly placed little cottage that he could imagine. The windows were shiny and clear. The porch was strong and intact. The steps where his footprints originated were whole and inviting.

It's beautiful... Seth watched the light shine through the windows as he bathed in the sweet sounds and smells of early summer that were in the air. He stared at the beach house, with no anger, no fear, and no questions. All of that was gone. He simply felt happy. He felt Love.

As he stared at the sunlight glistening off the windows, he noticed what appeared to be movement inside the house. It was only a split second, but he swore he saw someone walk by one of the windows. He took a step towards the beach house with a curious look on his face. Again he saw someone walk by the window and he stopped. He lifted his nose in the air slightly and began to smell wonderful aromas streaking across the sand and over to him. *Someone is cooking... I'm not alone...*

He looked down at his hand slowly and lifted it up to his face. The bright sunlight glistened off the ring on his finger. He knew immediately what it meant.

Sovannah!

He looked straight up into the sky and turned his face to the sun, once more lifting his arms wide, as if hugging the sunlight as it streamed across the water to his face. A single thought crossed his mind..... *I'm home.*

THE END